K IS FOR KINKY

Also by Alison Tyler

———

K IS FOR KINKY

EROTIC STORIES
EDITED BY ALISON TYLER

CLEIS
PRESS

Published in the United States by Cleis Press Inc.,
P.O. Box 14697, San Francisco, California 94114.

Printed in the United States.
Cover design: Scott Idleman
Text design: Karen Quigg
Cleis Press logo art: Juana Alicia
First Edition.
10 9 8 7 6 5 4 3 2 1

Acknowledgments

Kisses to:

Adam Nevill

Felice Newman

Frédérique Delacoste

Violet Blue

The Lust Bites Ladies

and SAM, always.

The difference between erotic and kinky:

Erotic is using a feather. Kinky is using the whole chicken.

—UNKNOWN COMEDIAN

contents

INTRODUCTION

NOW WHAT TURNS ME ON? What really makes me squirm in my seat? The unexpected. If a story takes a sharp turn to the right when all signs pointed left, that's what makes me cross my legs and start to rock. I've come up with a term for stories like this: *kinky*.

Kinky is being fucked while wearing a bumblebee costume, as in "Wings and All" by Emerald—

I heard my fishnets rip further, tearing along my inner thighs, and felt him push my black thong out of the way. My head went back against the bed as he shoved my thighs against my body and entered me. My shiny black heels bounced above his head as he fucked me harder than he ever had—as hard as I'd always wanted him to. But it was the unfamiliar carnal look in his eyes that almost made me come.

I ran my vinyl-covered fingers through his hair and held on tight, biting my lip to keep quiet. His roommate was downstairs, and it was my practice to be quiet when we fucked at his place. So it was silent as he took me, wings and all....

Kinky is being drawn on, as in Saskia Walker's ink-on-skin fantasy, "Sign Your Name":

He let go of her wrists, and lifted her skirt right up, exposing her. "Ooh, white cotton panties. Just like a blank page."

He ran the pen down the front of her panties, pushing both pen and fabric into the groove of her pussy. Her flesh blazed under that touch. She glanced down to look at the solid line he had drawn, but he was still moving the pen, pressing deeper into her groove, rolling over her clit. When she gave a sudden gasp, he paused and concentrated on the same spot, drawing back and forth over it. A jaggedy blue scribble was forming right over the spot.

And kinky is being turned into an automated fuck toy for your lover's pleasure, as in Jerry Jones' "Coin Operated":

His hands trembled as she stretched her leg forward and gently massaged his cock with her foot until he groaned and leaned back, all thoughts of covering his nudity forgotten. As he brought the clamp closer to the sensitive nub of flesh on his chest, she started rubbing harder. He opened the clamp and she slid her foot under him to gently massage his balls as well. The clamp embraced his nipple and his excited moans turned to a hiss of pain.

But mostly, kinky is the way I felt when I read each of these sinful stories for the first time, free hand snaking down under my skirt as I flipped the pages one by one.

XXX,
Alison

saskia walker

sign your name

KIND OF WEIRD, that's how Molly thought of herself. She told guys that, but mostly they thought she was referring to her attitude or her dress sense, both of which were also kind of weird. She was skittish and wayward, punky, yet quiet and thoughtful. And it wasn't just that. The thing that got Molly off sexually was pretty unusual too, and she felt it was only fair to let potential lovers know what she needed, up front. The only way to do that was to show them how it worked. Mostly, they didn't take her seriously. That is, not until Doug came along.

Doug had a spark of curiosity in his bright blue eyes, and a warm, subtle sense of humor. He was intuitive. She liked the way he looked, had done since the day he first walked into her workplace. He had cropped and spiked black hair, and smiled slow and long, kind of like Mickey Rourke. He ran the secondhand music exchange down the street, and he chose quiet times to come and collect his dry cleaning from the outlet where she worked, times when he remembered that she'd be working her shift—and was just about to shut up shop. He brought her black Nubuck leather jeans, and a multitude of cool Dragonfly shirts, shirts he wouldn't trust to his beat-up old washing machine— or so he said. She'd already warmed to him when he began to chat her up more purposefully.

"You know, Molly," he said, leaning over the countertop to close the gap between them, "we get on so well. Maybe we could go for a drink sometime." He smiled that drawn-out smile, and it made something inside her tick hopefully.

She put her pen down on the countertop between them, making a line in the space there, and nodded. "Okay."

"Great. Give me your number and we can work out a time." He picked up the pen and flipped over his till receipt, ready to write on the back of it.

Molly stared at the pen in his hand, immediately aroused and self-aware. The key to her kink was right there in his hand. She liked to be written on—in fact it aroused her to the point where she could come from that act alone. This was the time to show him; then she could see how he would react.

She took a deep breath. "Tell you what…" Her voice sounded shaky, and she hated that. She didn't want this to go wrong. She wanted him. Badly. "Why don't you give me your number? It'll be better that way. Really, I promise."

Before he could question her, or show doubt about why she'd said that, she shoved her forearm out across the counter between them, pulling up the sleeve of her top. She ran her finger up and down the soft, sensitive skin on the inside of her forearm. "Write it...here. Please."

Would he laugh at her? One corner of his mouth was still lifted and stayed that way. He toyed with the pen, his eyes assessing. Her breath was trapped in her throat. A moment later, he slowly moved one hand and held her wrist down on the counter with it, while he began to write on the spot she had indicated with the other.

His hand around her wrist was warm and strong and sure. And then—oh. The pressure he applied through the ballpoint on her skin made her nerves leap, the sensation chasing itself up her arm and through her body, flooding her with arousal. She bit her lip.

He looked up from the place he was writing and back at her. She could tell he'd sensed this wasn't just about exchanging numbers. A needy moan escaped her lips.

He stared; one eyebrow lifted, the pen, also. "Did I hurt you?"

"No." She could barely get that one small word out, and when she did, it was with a breathless, relieved sigh. She shrugged. "I'm wired weird. I just wanted you to know. Up front."

She snatched her arm away, bracing herself for the disbelieving laughter, the snide remark. Tension hung in the air between them, seemingly endless. Then he looked down at the countertop. What was he thinking?

He glanced up. "Kinky girl, huh?"

She stared him directly in the eye, her heart beating fast as she braced herself for rejection. "Does it bother you?"

"Quite the opposite," he replied, and flashed her a grin. "If I know what turns you on, it gives me power...and it just so happens I like to be in charge."

Oh, that made her hot. It was so far from what she had expected him to say, so direct. And then he moved. In a heartbeat, he levered himself over the counter, jumping lithely down onto her side of it. For the first time, he had breached the physical divide between them—and he'd brought the pen with him. Holding it raised in his hand, he put his free hand on her shoulder and walked her through the rails of plastic-covered clothes, backing her toward the wall behind those rails, out of sight of the shop front. He cornered her up against the wall.

Her body pulsed with the thrill of his actions.

He grasped her two hands easily in one of his, and lifted her chin with the pen under her jaw, an action that shot sensation down her neck and chest, right into her hardening nipples. She gasped for breath, her eyes closing and her head moving back to lean against the wall.

"Oh yes, it really does it for you, doesn't it? How bad is it?"

He still had the pen under her jaw, controlling the position of her head and where she could look. Could she tell him? Her eyes were shut and she kept them that way. "I need it." Her voice was a mere murmur. "I can't come any other way, not the way I do if…"

When her voice trailed off, he moved the pen just enough to apply pressure to the sensitive flesh beneath her jaw. Her eyes flashed open.

"Is this making you wet?"

"Yes." He was close, staring at her, his eyes bright and focused. The curiosity she had sensed in him had multiplied. He was aroused by her responses, his body shifting close against hers, one knee pressed against the wall at the side of her body.

He gave a soft chuckle. "You know, Molly, I used to wonder about you. I liked the way you looked, very pretty but different, and always thinking...always with the sexy eyes. There was something else though, wasn't there? You were always playing with your pen, always sucking on the end of it. Couldn't just be ready for the next customer, I figured. Couldn't quite work out what it was, but it made me hard just watching you play with the damn thing." His voice turned husky, right at the end there.

"Are you hard now?" She flashed her eyes, her responses rolling out readily.

His grip on her wrists tightened and he moved the back of her contained hands against the zipper on his jeans. "Well, what do you think?"

Beneath the black denim he wore, his cock was rigid.

Her skin tingled with awareness when he brushed it over that spot. She nodded. He moved the pen, lifting it from beneath her jaw and taking it down to the hem of her miniskirt. Putting it under the fabric and between her thighs, he tapped it from side to side then up and down, making her thighs tremble with the need for a deeper mark, the pressure, and the stain—the written evidence on her body.

He let go of her wrists, and lifted her skirt right up, exposing her. "Ooh, white cotton panties. Just like a blank page."

She stepped from one foot to the other, wired. "You're torturing me," she breathed.

"Maybe this will help." He ran the pen down the front of her panties, pushing both pen and fabric into the groove of her pussy.

Her flesh blazed under that touch. She glanced down to look at the solid line he had drawn, but he was still moving the pen, pressing deeper into her groove, rolling over her clit. When she gave a sudden gasp, he paused and concentrated on the same spot, drawing back and forth over it. A jaggedy blue scribble was forming right over the spot.

"You like that?"

Her clit was swollen and pounding, the direct stimulation hitting her hard. She nodded. "Very much."

He did it some more.

Her hands and head were flat to the wall, her hips jutting out toward him. "Oh yes, yes," she said, pounding the palm of one hand against the wall as she came, her free hand reaching out for his shoulder to steady herself.

She was about to speak, to say thank you, to say something, when she heard the door opening in the shop front, and hurriedly pulled her skirt straight. He stepped to one side, pointing down with the pen he held, possessively. "I want those panties, you better keep them for me."

"Maybe." She smiled. She wanted them, too. "You only gave me half of your number," she added, concerned that he might leave now.

He spanked her on the behind playfully, smiling that smile of his. "Fuck that. You're coming home with me tonight."

A month later, Molly's foible had been well and truly exploited. Before Doug, she'd fretted about her route to sexual pleasure. Doug had all but mended that in her, and now he was adding his own spin. He was fascinated with her odd little needs, and he'd written on just about every part of her body, watching her, enjoying her—wanking with one hand or fucking her hard while he gave her exactly what she wanted. Afterward, he tended her carefully, bathing her and massaging away the telltale signs of her kink.

That made her feel cherished, safe.

He asked her to move in with him. She said she'd think about it. He didn't press her on the subject. Instead, he showed her that those kind-of-weird needs of hers would never be forgotten.

That night he took her back to his place and told her he was going to kick it up a notch. The way he said it scared her and thrilled her at the same time.

Shortly after, she found herself naked and blindfolded, standing with her back against the wall, her hands splayed either side of her— just as he had instructed. Keyed up to the max, she shifted anxiously, unable to stay still. She'd never been blindfolded before, but the velvet covering her eyes was soft as a sigh, a shield that raised the awareness of her every other sense. Her body ached for contact, for pleasure and relief.

She could sense him moving.

The room was silent and the air was still, but she knew he was treading softly, watching her and making a plan. That was his way. Maybe she'd sensed that in him when she'd watched him across the counter. It was his curiosity, and his intensity, that had spiked her interest. Rightly so, as it turned out.

She heard a click and a fan whirred into action. A moment later the air brushed over her alert skin, tantalizingly. A whimper escaped her.

He began to hum under his breath, then he sang to her huskily. A song she loved. A song from ages ago. Breathless, aroused laughter escaped her; she felt delirious under his spell. "Dougie, please, you're playing with me."

"Always, sweetheart, but you love that."

He was so right. She squeezed her thighs together, scared to say more, and scared to ruin this.

"Will it drive you mad, not being able to see where I choose to write on you?"

"I don't know." She swallowed. "Maybe." She turned her face away, desperate with longing for that first touch, the pressure she craved— her skin was crawling with the need for it. Watching him write on her was half the pleasure, she thought. Not seeing it was an unknown quantity. But Doug knew and understood that, and—now—so did she.

Slowly, he drew a line around each wrist.

Her arms trembled with the sheer intensity of sensation that shot along the surface of her skin, and deeper.

"Shackles." His voice was a murmur close to her. "Because I want you to be mine." He kissed her throat and then, slowly, with great deliberation, he signed his name right across her breastbone.

"Oh. Oh, oh," she cried. The intense sensation shot beneath her skin, wiring her whole body into the experience. Her nipples were hard and hurting. She shuddered with arousal, her toes curling under, her heart thudding against the wall of her chest.

His next move came out of nowhere. He drew along the crease at the top of one thigh, then the other. The sudden deep stimulation in a place so sensitive primed her for release. She longed to see his marks on her.

"The insides of your thighs are wet, right down to here." There was admiration in his voice. Restraint, too. He touched her with the pen, briefly, between her thighs, and it made her squirm up against the wall.

"Face the wall," he instructed, his voice husky.

She turned.

His cock brushed against her buttock. "There's a box to your left, step onto it."

She moved her foot, felt her way. He guided her up onto the box.

"Offer yourself to me."

Understanding hit her; he was going to fuck her there up against the wall, while she stood there on a box, blindfolded. This was Doug; this is how he liked to have her, to be in charge of her. Hands braced against the wall, she spread her feet, angling her bottom up and out.

"Oh yes, I like you this way, on a pedestal, all ready for me." His cock moved between her thighs.

The box put her right at the height he needed to glide up into her. Anticipation had her in its grip. She was breathing so fast she felt dizzy. Picturing the shackles he had drawn on her wrists, she splayed her fingers on the wall, knowing she'd need to anchor herself—he got kind of wild when he was inside her. He was humming again now, and she wondered what he'd done with the pen. Was it in his mouth while he arranged her to his satisfaction?

He stroked her pussy, opening her up. His fingers moved with ease, slick, sliding in against her wetness. With two digits, he opened her up to his cock. The intensity of being felt, held, and displayed that way on a pedestal all at once took her breath away. With one hand around her hips, he thrust the thick shaft of his erection inside her.

Where is his other hand? The thought echoed around her mind frantically.

Then she found out.

Even as he thrust into her, in shallow quick maneuvers, keeping her in place, he began to write down her spine with his free hand.

It was almost too much. Her shoulders wriggled and her pussy twitched on his shaft. Her stomach flipped and sweat broke out on her skin. She would have staggered, if he hadn't got her pinned by his cock. She panted out loud, her mouth opening, her body clenching on him rhythmically.

"Oh yes, that's good," he said, keeping the pen moving in around her spine, working his way down her back. "This makes you so wild, you're going to squeeze my cock until I come."

"Can't control it," she whispered, head hanging down.

"That's the way I like it," he grunted.

By the time the pen reached her tailbone, she was a panting wreck on the verge of climax. He drew a wobbly heart there at the base of her spine, following the shape around and around with his pen. The action and her response were mesmerizing, and when her climax hit it lasted long, easing off only to return in a rush when he grew rigid and jerked, coming deep inside her.

They stayed that way until his cock finally slid free, and then he untied the blindfold and lifted her into his arms, carrying her toward the bathroom.

She squinted up at him, clinging to him. Kissing his shoulder, his throat, and when he turned toward her, his mouth, she felt grateful to have found her perfect opposite. She was still trembling from the intensity of her release.

"This is one of my favorite parts, scrubbing you down afterward, my dirty girl."

"It gets you going again," she teased, smiling at him.

"You're not wrong there."

Inside the bathroom, he stood her on the bath mat, and reached for the taps. While the bath filled, he traced his finger across her chest, following the line of his name that he had written there earlier. "So, you'll move in with me?"

She shivered, an echo of her orgasm tingling from the core of her body to the tip of her spine. "Yes."

"Good," he replied, nonchalantly. "Ever thought about having a tattoo?"

She saw the humor in his eyes. He hadn't made a big deal of her moving in, just as he hadn't made a big deal about her kink that first day. He'd come to understand her, very quickly. "Having a tattoo would probably kill me, and you know it," she replied.

"Hell of a way to go, though," he mused, as he lifted her into the bath.

The warm water moved in and around her legs and hips, melting her. After he scrubbed her down, he would climb in with her. That was one of her favorite parts.

He kneeled down beside the bath and reached for the sponge. "If you ever do have a tattoo, I want to be the one who is inside you while you're having it done. Is that a deal?"

She reached her hand around his head, drawing him in for a kiss. "It's a deal," she whispered.

MARKED

NOWING WHAT I DO NOW about Mark and his tricks, it's ironic that his shoulders were what first got my attention. They were a luscious pair of deltoids, firm and curvy and all wrapped up in smooth bronzed skin. He was wearing swim trunks—we met at my friend Diana's pool party—and I quickly noticed the rest of him was easy on the eye as well.

I snagged Diana as she was passing with a tray of margaritas. "So, who's Mr. Muscles?" I asked coolly, not letting on that my bathing suit was already a little damp *down there* and I hadn't even dipped a toe in the water.

"The guy by the diving board? He's my personal trainer, Mark Jarrett. He owns Make Your Mark Fitness on Piedmont." She gave me a knowing smile. "I'd definitely go for it, Sophie. Believe me, Mark knows his stuff."

"I'm not his type. His upper body bulges are so much bigger than mine."

Diana snorted. "You've been too busy gawking at him to notice Mark's been giving you the eye, too. I'm going to put you two on barbecue duty together. If you want to get better acquainted with his shish kebab later, that's up to you." She wiggled her eyebrows and sashayed on to the next group of guests.

I sipped my second margarita as I considered my options. Diana seemed quite knowledgeable about Mark's bedroom talents. Not that it should interfere with my own scheme—this wouldn't be the first time she and I had done a share-and-compare with a cute guy.

The bigger problem was that he truly wasn't my type. I went for troubled intellectuals who got me all caught up in their mind games. I was still recovering from an affair with a religious studies professor who liked me to paddle him in his office while he cried and confessed his sins. Before that was a reedy poet who only got hard when we did it standing up in semipublic places. This Mark guy was so clean-cut and superficial. He was basically nothing more than a glorified gym teacher.

But maybe a quick bite of all-American boy meat was just what I needed. I'd snatch one night of selfish pleasure, then walk away. There'd be no attachments, no regrets. I'd make damn sure Mr. Muscles wouldn't make his mark on me.

I was grinning at my own joke when Mark himself happened to glance in my direction. He smiled back, his brown eyes glittering. If I didn't know better, I'd have said his expression was almost sly, as if he knew exactly what I was thinking and took it as a personal challenge.

I felt a little flutter in my belly, pure lust mingled with a different kind of excitement. I liked games. Especially this kind, where I made the rules and was sure to win.

I woke up to the whir of a blender and the scent of mango drifting from the kitchen. Where the hell was I? With my first yawn it came back to me: this was Mark's place, his rumpled futon, his condom lying in the wastebasket next to me. I remembered laughing with him as we basted the kebabs, then dancing at a club until the wee hours. Later somehow we were sinking onto his futon, and Mark was pulling me on top of him and whispering that I should do whatever felt good for me, because it all felt so good for him. And after that, I recalled— I blushed a little to think of it—my moans as I climaxed on his cock.

I smiled into the pillow, reveling in the victory. Although I rarely came the first time with a guy, something about straddling Mark's toned belly and riding him just the way I liked had done the trick. In fact, the sex had been everything I wanted: selfish, purely physical, and very satisfying.

"Hey, Sophie, you're up. Would you like to try my special mango smoothie? All my clients say it's a great way to start the day."

I was beginning to wonder exactly what sort of personal training Mark was in the business of providing, but his smile was so sweet I could hardly refuse. I wasn't so sure about his next offer though—a wake-up massage. At this point in the game I was supposed to be heading home to carve a notch on my bedpost and forget this all happened.

Mark seemed to sense the cause of my hesitation. "Come on, it's just a back massage. It doesn't have to lead to anything more."

I shrugged and turned over on my stomach. It was Sunday, I didn't have any plans, why not let the guy service me in a different way? Mark popped open a bottle of coconut oil and within moments I was floating in an island paradise.

To his credit, he was doing a serious, professional job. No surreptitious butt groping, no tickling fingers creeping around to my breasts. And yet, the power in his hands, the knowing way he kneaded and stroked my flesh, was turning me on more than if he had tried to cop a few cheap feels. It would still count as a one-night stand if I added in a quick morning-after fuck, right?

I turned on my back and gave him a seductive smile.

He smiled back, those amber eyes melting into me.

Shit, I think this guy actually likes me.

This wasn't part of the plan at all, but I wasn't going to panic. I hooked my hand around his neck and pulled him down for a kiss. The rest would follow naturally. We'd fuck, say thanks, and go our separate ways.

But Mark had other ideas.

Just when I'd settled on top of him, he put his hands on my hips and tilted me back to an upright position so my ass was resting on his thighs. "Have you ever tried the Princess Position? It's a nice variation for ladies who like to be on top."

"What is that, some Kama Sutra thing?"

"I think it's a Mark Jarrett original. You strengthen your midback muscles and your gluts at the same time you're having fun."

Okay, so he had me curious. I was as time crunched as the next woman; why not get two workouts in one?

"Sit up straight, shoulders down," he continued in his bossy, gym teacher tone. "You slouch a little, you know. I noticed that yesterday. It's subtle but I can show you how to fix it. Tighten your gluts and tuck your tail. That's right. Can you feel how that opens the chest?"

It felt sort of perverted getting a lecture on my posture while I was impaled on his cock, but Diana said he charged a hundred bucks an hour at the gym, so I wasn't about to complain about free training. Besides, every time I squeezed my ass, my cunt muscles gripped his cock tighter, which got me feeling very warm and tingly in no time.

"See, you look like a princess now. Proud and beautiful."

"It feels like I'm showing off my tits," I confessed, then regretted it.

"You have lovely breasts. You *should* show them off."

He began caressing my shoulders lightly with his fingertips. I shivered. I'd never realized what an erogenous zone they were.

"Don't slouch. See, you're doing it again. Pay attention to your posture. I'll do the rest."

He tweaked my nipple. I gasped and instinctively curled forward, but immediately rolled my shoulders back and tucked my pelvis as if in answer to his unspoken command.

"Good job, princess," he murmured and continued to play with my nipples, flicking and pinching them gently, rubbing them in slow circles with spit-moistened palms.

My whole torso was on fire and I wanted more than anything to fall forward, jam my tit between his warm, wet lips and rub my clit against his hard belly like last night. But strangely enough, I liked it this way, too. I liked the way my breasts jutted out, the nipples taut and red, shamelessly accepting his homage. I liked the way the constriction in my shoulders and ass made me feel like I was wrapped up in some kinky full-body corset, forcing my desire deeper inside me, a throbbing, molten star waiting to explode.

"That's right, princess, keep your shoulders back. We're almost there."

In spite of the praise, I wasn't acting much like a proper princess anymore. My chest was flushed pink with arousal, beads of sweat trickled down my chest and sides, and I was whimpering. When Mark slipped a finger between my lips and began to rub my clit with quick come-hither strokes, any attempt at royal decorum was futile. I flung my head back and howled as my orgasm finally burst free, spiraling up my spine like a fireball as my ass jerked and quivered over him.

Mark didn't protest when I collapsed over him in a gelatinous heap, although at that point my posture left much to be desired.

"It's your turn," I croaked, my throat sore from the screaming.

"I'll wait," he said, stroking my back, "until I make you come the second time."

For a woman, meaningless one-night stands are always a gamble— you can end up the loser even if you win. But this time I knew, as I grinned into his hunky shoulder, that I'd just hit the jackpot.

Two weeks later, I'd pretty much moved in with Mark, although we weren't officially a couple, at least in my mind. I had to admit there were benefits to the arrangement: the smoothies, the free workout advice, the fact I could laugh and relax with him because it didn't really mean anything. Best of all, I discovered that Mark enjoyed games as much as I did, if I nudged him in the right direction.

Like the evening Mark was watching an NBA playoff game and I sat down beside him to snuggle while I read over some proposals I'd brought home from work. He slipped an arm around me and gave my shoulder a friendly squeeze. I'm not sure why, but suddenly work was the last thing on my mind. I had to fuck Mark, the sooner the better. I burrowed a little closer and rested my hand on his thigh. He smiled at me, absently, then turned his gaze back to the TV.

I shifted restlessly. If I wasn't even calling him a boyfriend, I hardly had the right to demand his attention when the fate of his favorite team was in the balance. I'd just about resigned myself to an evening of dutiful reading when his fingers tightened around my shoulder again.

I held my breath.

Eyes still glued to the TV, Mark's left hand crept over to unbutton the top button of my blouse.

The hand withdrew as he pumped a fist in the air for a three-pointer.

I waited, my chest rising and falling in shallow gasps, until the hand returned.

With aching slowness, Mark worked his way down the column of buttons, until the blouse hung open to expose my lacy bra. He cupped my breast, his fingers kneading lightly, but without real focus. He wasn't even hitting the good parts. I sighed loudly and shuffled the papers in my lap.

Finally he turned to me. "What's the matter, princess?"

As if he didn't know. With this attitude, he didn't deserve sex, but suddenly I was feeling hornier and more desperate than ever. "Please, Mark. Can we...you know?"

He shrugged and looked back at the TV, his expression blank. "I'm happy just doing this for a while."

His fingers started up with the teasing again. This time he did graze my nipple now and then, but it wasn't enough. In frustration, I unzipped my jeans and wiggled them down to my knees, then shoved my hand in my panties and started to masturbate.

At last I got him to peel his eyes away from the TV, although he glanced back to watch a free throw. I quickened the pace and moaned. His eyes fell to my lap again. This time they lingered. Mark had asked me to play with myself for him our first morning together, but I'd felt too shy. This time I pulled out the stops, squirming and jerking my hips and murmuring how much I wanted a big, hard cock inside me. It wasn't a lie. I was so wet, my finger made a moist, squishy sound as I strummed.

Mark made a funny grunt and clicked off the TV. Resting his hands on my shoulders, he eased me back on the sofa as if he were positioning my body for an exercise. Then, with the same deliberation, he peeled off my panties and climbed on top, bending my right leg up to my shoulder, the perfect stretch for the lower back and hamstring.

"Don't you want to see who wins?" I whispered, perversely, for I was sure I'd go crazy if he did actually stop to watch the game again.

"I already know, Sophie. It's you, right?" The mischievous glimmer in his eyes might have given me pause if I hadn't been busy thrusting my ass up to get him so deep inside me the pleasure edged into delicious pain. All that mattered now was that I'd won this battle. There'd be plenty of time later to worry about the war.

One month after the pool party, I finally went "out" with Mark for the first time to a trendy sake bar with Diana and Josh. It wasn't a date. In spite of the great sex, I told myself, Mark and I were still strictly no-strings.

For an hour or two, I actually believed it was true.

Then, between the entrée and dessert, Mark put his arm around me, gave my shoulder a squeeze and whispered, "You're slouching again, princess. Shoulders back."

My eyes shot open and I could barely restrain a cry of dismay. Because immediately after he said those words, my underwear was soaked.

"Excuse me," I mumbled and dashed off to the ladies' room, praying it hadn't seeped through to my skirt. In the stall, I slipped my fingers into my panties and sure enough, I was as slick as if he'd played with me for half an hour. Without even thinking, I started rubbing and literally, in thirty seconds, I was coming, biting back my moans as my body shuddered against the metal partition.

The bathroom door swung open. "Sophie?" It was Diana. "Hey, I know what happened out there."

My heart leaped in my chest. How could she know? Did Mark do this to her, too?

"I've got extra tampons if you need any."

I breathed a sigh of relief. "Thanks, but I have some."

"Of course, you always plan ahead. By the way, you and Mark make a cute pair."

I was about to protest that we were not a "pair," thank you, but I realized the only thing I really wanted was to get Mark's cock inside me for my encore orgasm.

That's when it hit me. My glorified gym teacher was cleverer than I ever imagined.

I marched out to the table and announced that I wasn't feeling well and had to go home early. Mark was all solicitation and concern as he followed me out to the car, but as soon as we had the doors closed, I let him have it.

"Drive to that motel down the street. I'll wait in the car while you get us a room."

He turned to me, eyebrows raised.

"Don't look innocent. You knew what you were doing to me from the beginning."

He smiled smugly. "I guess it worked then."

"Like a charm. And now you're going to make me come again, because you got me so turned on with your secret signal I already came once in the restroom. It took less than a minute. I'm a model trainee, aren't I?"

"The best."

Once he got us the room and the door had closed behind us, I pushed him down on the bedspread, yanked down his pants and straddled him. Pulling aside the elastic of my panties, I slid onto his cock with a groan.

"Touch my shoulder. Say the words."

I wasn't sure if it was an order or a plea, but Mark obliged by squeezing my shoulder gently. My pussy responded with a gush of juices and I started to ride him, our bodies making soft, kissing sounds together.

"Mind your posture now, princess," he whispered, his lips curved up in a triumphant grin. "You'd better be good, because you never know when I'll strike. Maybe it will be at a party next time. I'll give you the signal and you'll be so turned on you'll have to rush to the powder room to masturbate. Or maybe I'll follow you and fuck you on the bath mat with your knees pushed to your shoulders because I know you like it deep. You'll do whatever I say because you're marked now, Sophie. You're mine."

As I ground my hips into him, teetering on the edge of climax, I knew Mark was right. He did have me in his power. He'd trained my body to respond to him like some groveling sex slave, which was the last thing I'd had in mind when I met him. And yet, in my own way, I'd won, too.

I'd finally found myself the kind of kinky bastard I could get attached to after all.

MATHILDE MADDEN

NOT TONIGHT

KNOCKING ON HER DOOR was always the most frightening part. His heart hammered, just as it always did. He swallowed gently and stood up straight, just as he always did. But when she opened the door, everything was different.

"Not tonight," she said, without any sign of regret. And then the door closed again.

Taken aback, he stood for some time, staring at the wood grain of her front door; not quite able to believe it. Steeling himself—finally—with something that was more desperate desire than real courage, he took hold of the door handle and turned. It wasn't locked.

Uninvited and uncommanded he walked into her hallway. "What did you say?" he called, sounding far sharper than he meant to, than he would have dared to.

There was no reply. So he went to find one.

He found her in the study; in half dark. The only light in the room came from a small lamp on the desk, which was making a pool of light on her paperwork and sparkling glints in her hair and the rims of her spectacles.

She didn't even look up. "I said 'Not tonight.' " He could hear her gritted teeth. "It's just not a good time."

He stepped into the room and pushed the study door closed behind him. This place looked so ordinary, even in semidarkness, and yet this was the room she also used as his torture chamber. There was the corner where she would make him stand and face the wall, his trousers lowered so she could see the marks her cane had left. And under that covered table he knew there was a cage, which was too small and caused cramps in his long limbs and muscular shoulders. It was too dark to see the iron rings that she had had sunk into the walls months ago, high enough that if she manacled his wrists to them he would be forced up onto tiptoes.

In this room of all places, it was impossible for him to let it go. "But it's Wednesday," he said.

She still didn't look up from her desk. "I know perfectly well what day of the week it is."

"Sorry." He creased his brow. He felt himself growing more petulant by the minute. It was all he could do not to stamp his foot. Stamp his foot or get down on his knees. "What's wrong?"

She sighed and finally looked up at him. The light caught her face then, and he caught his breath. "Nothing, I'm just tired. I don't have the energy tonight." She did look tired.

He cocked his head and fixed his coyest expression. He lived for Wednesday nights. Work had been hell these last few months and he didn't think he could bear to trudge back into London without some kind of tension release. "You don't have to do anything," he said, very gently. "I'll wait on you. Please."

"I said 'No.' "

He swallowed and moved closer to the desk until he was near enough to rest his palms on the top. "But why? You know you want to."

She held his gaze. "Don't tell me what I want. You are really pushing your luck now."

"Am I? What are you going to do about that?" He lifted one knee onto the desktop and lowered his gaze, deferent and needy and hard. Ready.

Her expression was unreadable. "Do you take me for some kind of fool? I told you. Now leave."

"Make me," he hissed, hoping that this banging heart wasn't audible as he raised his other knee, and gingerly climbed up to kneel on her desk.

She fixed his gaze with flashing eyes as their faces drew level. "No."

"You want to though, don't you? Listen to how I'm talking to you." He gulped quickly. "Surely you can't let it go unpunished. You can't tell me you don't want to hear me scream right now."

"Is that a fact?" And then, just as he thought he might have to give up, came a tiny half smile, just a flash that was thought better of, but a flash nonetheless. She was teasing back, even if she didn't mean to, and he rose to the challenge.

"Oh you know it is. You really ought to beat me. You ought to beat me harder than you did last week. What you did to me last week was…" He paused while he searched for the perfect word. "Last week

— 27 —

was amazing. Although I don't know how I bore it. I was almost at my limit. The marks lasted for three days, you know. I could barely sit down. It's a good job my boss wasn't around to wonder why I was using the mantelpiece as a desk."

He allowed himself a little internal smile as he saw her pupils dilate a little.

"Really?" Her voice had a little shake to it now. "You couldn't sit at your desk?"

He knelt up on the desk and took hold of his collar, opening the top button, suggestively. "No, I couldn't, I was far too sore." He popped open another button. Then another.

"Well it's a good job you like frustration," she said, taking his hands and stopping him before he undid the fourth button, "because I have no intention of hurting you, tonight…."

Barely before she finished speaking he pushed her hands away from his shirt, leaning across the desk and placing a pale finger across her lips. "Because you'd rather be using me?" He punctuated the question with a flash of raised eyebrow and a slow smile. "Perhaps you'd prefer me on my knees tonight. Taking off your knickers with my teeth—because you know that my tongue works so much better if my wrists are bound behind my back. If I'm helpless as you tear at my hair and force me against you, raping my face until you are satisfied. Jerking your hips against me so I know for certain that you own me. That I know for certain I'm yours and I come all over the floor without even touching myself. Like the filthy bastard I am."

She reached out and took his hand gently, pushing it away from her lips. "Well it seems you have even more of a talented tongue than

I ever realized. I can't imagine who taught you to talk like that, though. You must be getting out and about in the big city."

"Oh no, I never go out. I stay at home every night and think of you. No one else has shaped my desire."

"Really, well I must make a note to leave you ungagged next time we play so you can put that verbal talent to good use. But not tonight. You know you really do need to learn restraint."

"Teach me about restraint then. If I'm bothering you, you know how you can stop me. Tie me up out of your way, chain me to the bed, lock me in your broom cupboard, strip me and cage me and leave me until morning. Make me an object. Make me your property. Own me. Oh God, please."

There was a breathless pause, and when she spoke again her voice was very low. "You know, you don't need to do this to make me want you."

He blinked, but continued his pleading, his voice cracking now with desperation and desire. "You don't have to tie me then. I don't need ropes or chains or bars to obey, give me the order and I'll face the wall until morning. Please. I don't need to come, I don't even need to touch you, but please. I just need you to own me."

She stared at him, a distant look in her eyes.

"I'll do anything. Anything you want. No safeword."

She held up both her hands. "Stop, please. It's not you. You've done nothing wrong. Do you think I'm tired of you? I could never grow tired of you. I need to…" She trailed off. "Just not tonight."

He stared at her. He tried to do that intense look that she seemed to find so easy, and he said again, "Please. I'll do anything."

"Anything?"

"Anything."

"Then go home."

MICHELLE HOUSTON

WANDERING WHERE LED

KAROLYN GAVE A QUICK JERK to the reins, drawing Wandering Scotsman to a stop as her host walked toward her, arms wide. "Karolyn, *bella*!" He kissed her cheeks and stepped back, holding her hands in his. "I'm so delighted you decided to grace us with your presence, and with your prized stallion."

Behind her, the stallion snorted and tossed his head, shaking his red mane at the attention. Smothering her smirk at his antics, she gave another tug to his reins to show her disapproval. Ian, or the Wandering Scotsman as he was called when in full regalia, neighed softly in response, acknowledging the silent chastening.

"So, where is the mare you wanted my Scotsman to cover?"

Her fellow Dominant dropped her hands and motioned to one of the stable attendants waiting behind him. The naked woman's leather heels tapped on the hardwood floor as she moved deeper into Aaron's stable. Hardcore into pony play, he had built the special stable on his property and routinely had anywhere from twenty to forty Dominants and subs running around, acting out their own fantasies. The curious, those who were tempted but uncertain, were able to play the role of attendants, performing menial, and often sexual, tasks requested of them.

Karolyn often wondered if some of the ponies actually slept in their stalls, as some had lavish beds and others simply contained padded tables and benches.

"Actually, *ma chère*, it's Daddy's Toy I want him to mount." The attendant returned, leading a young male, his long blond hair carefully braided and tied back, revealing striking features. "He's been fighting the bit, not adjusting as quickly as I would prefer. I want him to truly get the full experience."

Karolyn's breath caught at the idea. She had allowed Ian to mount, and thanks to strap-on be mounted by, several other submissives—all mares. As far as she knew, he had never been with another man, but the idea intrigued her. From the silence behind her, she knew he was considering the idea as well. He would have whinnied or shifted away if the idea repulsed him. As her gaze trailed over the approaching stallion, she could see the appeal. Daddy's Toy barely stood as tall as his attendant, who couldn't be more than five-eight, with delicate features.

When the stallion reached them, Aaron took the lead from the attendant and dismissed her back to her corner. "So, *bella,* what do you think?"

Karolyn shrugged, trying to be nonchalant when inside she was trembling with excitement. "If Daddy's Toy accepts him, then I have no problem with the arrangement." They both looked at the blond stallion.

His nostrils were flared, and his blue eyes sparkled with excitement as they traced over Ian's muscular frame.

She knew what he saw had to be tempting. Ian's long red hair, creamy skin, and athletic body turned many heads wherever they went.

Aaron led his stallion to the stall, and Karolyn followed at a slower pace, leading her Wandering Scotsman, giving him time to prepare himself mentally. As they watched, Aaron guided Daddy's Toy right up to a small padded table that stood chest high on him. Another attendant stepped into the room, his cock hard and colored a dusky red thanks to a cock ring. As Karolyn led her Scotsman further into the room, the attendant drew a step stool out of a cabinet and placed it at the base of the table, then grasped Daddy's Toy's lead.

With a click of his tongue, he coaxed the stallion onto the stool and leaned him over the padded table. Behind Karolyn, Ian started shifting from foot to foot. Reaching back, she grasped his cock and found it hard, his balls tight against his body. Her pussy clenched at the knowledge that he was as turned on by the idea of his covering another male as she was of allowing it to happen.

When the attendant finished lubricating the blond pony's anus, he turned to Karolyn. "Mistress, do you wish me to ring his cock?"

After giving her Scotsman's cock a squeeze, she nodded. The man dropped to his knees before Ian and pulled his cock into his mouth. After giving a few quick sucks, he pulled back and slipped the ring up Ian's cock. Almost immediately, his cock swelled, the veins popping out, the flesh turning a dark, angry red.

Reaching up, she unbuckled Ian's harness and pulled the bit from his mouth. She raised up on her toes and pressed her lips to his, then thrust her tongue into his mouth. Moving closer, she pressed her chest against him, even as she was aware of the attendant still kneeling at his feet, the back of his bald head trapped between their groins.

As she pulled back, she saw a familiar glazed look in Ian's eyes. Patting his cheek, she let him go. "Enjoy yourself," she whispered. Ian smiled and moved to stand behind the other stallion. Slowly, he ran his hands over the blond's legs and back, stroking softly and soothingly, until Daddy's Toy moaned in response.

Aaron moved to stand by his stallion's head and cupped his chin in his hands. When the attendant at her feet moved to stand, Karolyn lightly placed a hand over his shoulder and held him in place. If he really wanted to, he could have stood, but he sank back down. Idly, she stroked her fingertips over his shoulder as she watched her lover make his move.

Unlike Ian's tail, which was attached to a butt plug firmly planted in his ass, Daddy's Toy's tail was attached to a slender belt that encircled his hips. Ian shifted the blond's tail out of his way and grasping his cock in his hand, pressed it against the Toy's greased hole and thrust forward. Karolyn watched, breath held, as his cock disappeared inch by inch.

Her eyes widened as Aaron unzipped his pants and pulled out his cock. Daddy's Toy eagerly accepted it, slurping on it loudly as Ian started thrusting into his ass. Groans from all three men filled the room, sending a shiver through her body. Still stroking the attendant's shoulder, she pulled her skirt up, baring her pussy. The bald attendant buried his face against her pussy, his tongue stroking the seam of her pussy lips.

Karolyn dug her fingernails into the back of his head, grinding her pussy against his face. Her gaze locked on the action across the room, she widened her stance, allowing the attendant greater access. Almost immediately, his tongue thrust into her pussy, further exciting her.

The sway of the horse tail hanging from between Ian's clenched cheeks captured her attention. As he thrust into the blond's ass, his tail responded to the movements, swaying and jerking upright, almost like a horse in a trot. Inhaling deeply, she could smell the heady scent of male sweat and arousal.

Tightening her grip on the attendant's head, she slid her other hand between them to manipulate her clit. His nose brushed her knuckles as she plucked the tiny bud, increasing her own pleasure.

A loud moan drew her attention to Aaron in time to see him pull back and come. Karolyn's pussy clenched in response to the sight. The attendant was good with his tongue, but she suddenly craved a hard dick filling her.

Aaron leaned down, whispering to his stallion. Ian groaned and moments later, Daddy's Toy came, his milky cream splattering on the floor and the side of the table.

Out of nowhere, three more attendants silently entered the room. One moved to Aaron and knelt before him, sucking the Dominant's cock. Another freed Daddy's Toy and licked the still trickling come from his cock and then his face, while the third coaxed Wandering Scotsman away from the other stallion, stroking a moist cloth over his straining cock.

Karolyn could see the veins standing out in sharp contrast to his purplish-red skin. His gaze met hers. It was full of hunger for more and he silently pleaded for relief. While he watched, she ground her pussy against the attendant's face and climaxed, coating the bald man's face with her cream.

But rather than take the edge off, it only heightened her need. She grasped a handful of Ian's mane and led him out of the stall and into the empty one next door,

Kicking the door shut, she turned to face him. "Take off the ring," she demanded as she lifted her skirt again and moved to lean over the table. The leather felt cool and slick against her heated skin and bare pubic mound.

Glancing back over her shoulder, she found that Ian had obeyed and the ring was lying at his feet. She reached between her legs and parted her pussy lips with her fingers, demanding that he come closer.

Hesitantly, he complied, a questioning look in his eyes. They were both in foreign territory—had been ever since they arrived. Karolyn had never opened herself for him before, never assumed any kind of submissive stance.

"Mount me," she ground out, her pussy clutching in need. "Now, Wandering Scotsman, that was an order, not a fucking request."

The warm slide of his cock against her pussy felt so delicious she almost purred. As his head pushed into her core, the urge to purr turned into a soft scream at the intensity of the sensation.

He pounded into her, his body bent over her, his teeth nipping at her neck like a stallion would when mounting a mare. Struggling for control of the situation, she managed to command, "Don't come until I give you permission," before the ability to speak left her.

He was a stallion in rut, his body pressing her down into the padded table, holding her immobile as he savaged her. She shivered as his tail brushed the backs of her legs. With a gasp, she climaxed, her body undulating beneath him. She could hear Ian's harsh breath in her ears as he fought his own orgasm.

The image of the blond impaled on her lover's cock, rosy anus spread so deliciously for his girth, filled her mind. "My ass," she gasped, her pussy still gripping his cock from the intensity of her orgasm. "Fuck my ass."

Watching Wandering Scotsman cover mares had never excited her as much as seeing him with Daddy's Toy. Even when he had ridden Aaron's little Asian mare, Jade Empress, that hadn't turned her on as much. And then, she had whipped him while he did it, giving him a lash stroke for each thrust until she couldn't keep up with his rapid pace.

Ian shifted behind her and she felt his cockhead press against her. Instinctively, she clenched as he pressed forward, then hissed at the sting. She relaxed as she exhaled, and pushed back against him. It took some time, and tears were leaking from the corners of her eyes before he was fully seated. They were both panting from the exertions. As he began a thrusting motion, she buried three fingers in her pussy and rolled her thumb over her clit. With her other hand, she reached back and grabbed a handful of his hair.

He pounded into her, slamming her against the table, and she loved it. Moaning and screaming, whimpering and gasping, she thrilled in the animalistic rutting until her orgasm rushed up. Her pussy clenched tight on her fingers. With her last coherent thought, she told Ian, "Come when I do," then gave in to the sensations. Euphoria crashed over her as her body was wracked with the intensity of her climax. Dimly, she was aware of Ian's groan, then the moist heat of his come flooding her ass.

She sought to regain control of her breathing. As soon as she could think again, she opened her eyes and turned her head. In the mirror on the wall, she could see Ian hunched over her, his body trembling as the last traces of his orgasm rushed through him.

A soft knock on the door caused his head to jerk up.

"Go away, this room's occupied," Karolyn called out. Ian backed away and stood watching her as she rolled over and spread her legs.

"Well, you made a mess, now clean it up," she responded to his silent question. With a smile, he dropped to his knees and buried his face against her pussy, once more relinquishing control to her—like they both preferred.

As he lapped at her swollen and battered folds, Karolyn draped her legs over his shoulders and fisted her hands in his hair. He neighed against her pussy in response.

EMERALD

WIꞐGS anD ALL

K NOW WHAT YOU'RE GOING TO BE for Halloween yet?" Justin
asked me on the phone. When I'd last talked to him I'd been
trying to determine my costume for the Halloween party my best
friend had announced she was throwing tomorrow night.

"I'm going to be a bee," I informed him, grinning excitedly even
though he couldn't see me.

"A bee," he repeated. "That's…interesting." He sounded nonplused.

I was unfazed by his reaction. He didn't understand how adorable
my bee costume was because he hadn't seen it. When I'd spied the costume on one of my favorite lingerie websites the week before, I knew
the thing was mine. "You'll love it. I promise."

"If you say so." Justin sounded like he was smiling. I pictured his
smile, one of my favorite things about him. There were a lot of things
I loved about Justin: the way he looked, the way he watched me, the

way he spoke to me, the way he kissed me. There was only one problem on the horizon of our budding relationship, but I had to admit it was one that I was having a hard time ignoring.

"Maybe you can come over after the party to show me," he continued.

"Sure," I said casually. My friends who would be at the party had heard a little bit about Justin—to the point where they had dubbed him my "nice guy," as that apparently served as enough of a distinction to distinguish him from the other guys I had fucked. And therein, perhaps, lay the problem. I had no problem with Justin's "niceness," of course, but I had found that it overwhelmingly pervaded the one place I didn't necessarily want it to—which was in bed. Justin fucked sweetly. And he usually let me initiate things. Nothing wrong with that. But sometimes, I simply want to be thrown down and fucked. Fucked like I'm just there to provide pleasure for someone else. Fucked, to paraphrase the immortal words of Nine Inch Nails, like an animal.

But that wasn't the way Justin fucked.

I tuned back in abruptly as I realized he was talking again, telling me to stop by whenever I was done regardless of how late it was.

"Sure thing," I said. "See you tomorrow."

Twenty-four hours later, I stood in a towel, fresh out of the shower, collecting the accessories I had assembled to go with my costume: black thong, black fishnets, black vinyl thigh-high boots, black vinyl arm-length gloves. I spread them out on my bed along with the costume pieces and surveyed everything like I was checking the parts from the box before assembling a set of shelves.

I picked up the delicate pair of wings that were joined in the center by a fabric black-and-yellow-striped bee body. They were shaped with wire around the edges and filled with a fragile yellow mesh flecked with gold glitter that was already scattered dazzlingly on my floor. A black plastic headband sporting fuzzy yellow balls on springs served as feelers. I smiled as I pulled them out of their plastic wrapper. Then there was the costume itself—a smooth, black-and-yellow-striped tube top–style bodice ending at the hips, where it turned into a bright yellow multilayered tutu about eight inches long. It covered approximately half my ass.

I turned from the costume and sat at the vanity to do my hair, piling curls on top of my head before arranging the feeler headband among them with the care of a bride setting her veil. I smiled at the fuzzy bouncing feelers in the mirror above my mass of ringlets. Then, piece by piece I slid the costume on, ending by slipping my arms through the elastic loops attached to the wings. With a last glance in the mirror, I headed out the door.

The party was at my best friend Kennedy's house. I parked and got out of the car gingerly, careful not to catch my wings on the door frame. My fairly exposed fishnet-covered ass raised a few eyebrows at the party, but thankfully no one said anything. I knew this group wasn't used to seeing me like this—much as they may have been used to hearing about my various sexual exploits—but it was Halloween, so apparently I was afforded a few liberties. When Kennedy's husband Dave emerged from the kitchen and spotted me, he burst out laughing.

"I suppose I shouldn't be surprised that you managed to make a costume meant to represent an insect look like a fetish whore getup.

Why didn't you just pick something easy like a dominatrix or something?"

"You know I don't need Halloween to give me an excuse to dress like a fetish whore, David," I answered sweetly. "I just happen to think bees are awesome. Do you realize that the job of the queen bee is to basically get fucked by various boy bees all day long? Buzzing lovers who come in, do the job, and then fly away? I appreciate the chance to pay homage to such a brilliant species." I turned and smiled as Kennedy, dressed as an exotic witch, approached to offer me a miniature bag of candy corn from the plastic jack-o'-lantern she was carrying.

Greeting me with a hug, she said, "Somehow that wasn't exactly what I pictured when you told me you were going to be a bee." She looked me up and down with a smile. "I have to say, though, until tonight it would not have occurred to me that I would find a yellow tutu sexy. Well done." She looked back at me and winked. "Shame you're wasting it on us."

"Actually, I'm stopping at Justin's after I take off tonight."

"Oh, your nice guy," Kennedy recalled with a nod.

A few hours later I said goodnight and click-clacked my spiked heels down the sidewalk to my car. I arranged myself in the driver's seat, paying careful attention to my wings and ducking my head to keep the feelers out of the way while I closed the door. I checked my hair, which had kept its carefully curled placement during the party, and started the engine.

As I made my way to Justin's apartment, I fidgeted a little. My wings made driving a bit awkward, and the vinyl encasing my limbs was starting to make my skin feel hot. I was admittedly beginning to look forward to taking the whole thing off.

I parked and walked up to the apartment, entering when I heard a "Come in" in response to my knock. Justin's roommate Jake was on the couch watching TV; he laughed at my costume as I closed the door behind me.

"Hey, Elizabeth. Nice feelers," he said with a wink.

I smiled broadly at him and headed for the stairs that led up to Justin's room. The vinyl on my legs squeaked as I walked through his doorway. He looked up from his computer screen at me.

"Do you like it?" I turned around and looked over my shoulder, sensing my fuzzy yellow feeler springs bouncing as I craned to see the back of the frilly yellow tutu. I wiggled my hips and flipped it playfully, which wasn't really necessary because it didn't cover my ass even when it was placed properly. I beamed and turned my head back around, reaching for the elastic straps at my shoulders as I prepared to take the wings off.

Before I could, I felt Justin up against me from behind. Surprised, I started to turn, but he wrapped his arms around me, pinning my arms against my body and holding me in place as he softly kissed the side of my neck. I shivered. The wires of my wings pressed against my shoulder blades as Justin's hands moved slowly down my arms to my hips, where they snaked around to the front of me and glided up to my breasts. He hooked his fingers under the top of the black-and-yellow-striped elastic and slid it down, exposing my tits and immediately covering them with his hands.

Surprised, I tried to move again, but his body and arms held me in place. He moved from kissing my neck to my ear, still standing behind me. The unexpectedness of his actions made me breathless,

— 43 —

and I felt myself getting wetter with every move he made. I ran my hands over his, the ebony vinyl of my gloves shining in the dim light from his computer screen.

Justin pulled away slightly and spun me around, the black vinyl of my boots creaking as I moved. I caught my breath as he reached and cupped my crotch. My breathing continued in short gasps as he slowly maneuvered his fingers for a moment. Then his hand stilled; his eyes on mine, he suddenly gave a hard yank. Taken by surprise, I lurched forward against him as I heard the ripping of my fishnets. Immediately, I realized he had been maneuvering his fingers into their tiny holes to gain the leverage needed to tear them.

It worked. Obviously the wings weren't the only part of the costume that was delicate.

Pulling his cock out of his jeans, he grabbed a condom from the bedside table and had it on by the time he pushed me down on the bed, meeting my eyes in the darkness as he pressed himself on top of me and hooked his arms around the vinyl on my thighs. I heard my fishnets rip further, tearing along my inner thighs, and felt him push my black thong out of the way. My head went back against the bed as he shoved my thighs against my body and entered me. My shiny black heels bounced above his head as he fucked me harder than he ever had—as hard as I'd always wanted him to. But it was the unfamiliar carnal look in his eyes that almost made me come.

I ran my vinyl-covered fingers through his hair and held on tight, biting my lip to keep quiet. His roommate was downstairs, and it was my practice to be quiet when we fucked at his place. So it was silent as he took me, wings and all, on his bed in the dim light of the computer screen.

Justin got up on his knees, pulling my ankles to his shoulders and running his fingers lightly down the vinyl encasing my legs. He ran them all the way to my pussy, where he continued the motion until his fingers covered my clit, his blue eyes piercing mine, that same look in them relegating me to near-incomprehensible desire. He smiled slyly as he saw how close I was and knew how hard I was trying to be quiet. It had never been so difficult before. Then in a flash he was on top of me again, his fingers not breaking their rhythm as his lips found my ear.

"Go ahead, baby. The queen bee runs the show—I'm sure she's allowed to scream if she wants," he whispered.

His hot breath in my ear sent me over the edge, and I heard him chuckle as I cried out, shuddering, then gasping breathlessly as I lay in near-oblivion. Justin got back on his knees, slamming into me as I felt the rough glitter on my wings scraping against my back. He reached down and clutched my throat as I squeezed the yellow frills of my tutu with vinyl-clad hands. My head went back; I felt the springy feelers getting crushed between my head and the mattress. When he came, it was with a vengeance I hadn't seen before. His eyes squeezed shut, a harsh groan pushed through him as he slammed into me from above.

I watched his eyes as he opened them and looked into mine before pulling slowly back off me. Breathless, I eased myself into a sitting position, smoothing the front of my costume somewhat back into place.

Justin grinned at me, watching as I began to slide the wings off my shoulders. Shaking my head a little, I pulled the headband from my hair, now a mess of falling tendrils pasted with sweat to my neck. Justin leaned forward, licking the side of my neck, and I realized this was one buzzing lover the queen was going to keep.

JEREMY EDWARDS

SEDUCTION WITH A SPLASH

K ARA HAD TO PISS like nobody's business. *This could work out perfectly*, she thought. She had discovered long ago that flooding her panties was the best way at her disposal to seduce a certain kind of man. And she had also discovered, long ago, that she very much enjoyed doing it—so much that she often did it when there was no one around to seduce. Alone. Hot and dripping over her kitchen floor. Maybe it was kinky—okay, she had to admit it was *definitely* kinky—but Kara was making no apologies. It was a kink that repaid her in orgasms, time and again.

Now she was especially glad that she was headed toward Daniel's office, to drop in unexpectedly.

She shifted sensually in the driver's seat.

She knew that one type of guy would run screaming from a woman who was unabashedly pissing herself and expecting him to like it. But

Kara had discovered, long ago, that she could easily live without that type of guy.

Come here and wet upon me, beautiful lady. Contain yourself just long enough to walk briskly across this room and straddle my zippered lap. Mount me and wiggle into position...your ass, in sassy panties, pressing on my summer trousers, your short skirt draping down to tease my legs with its crisp edges. Then flood my lap, you gorgeous creature, let me feel your wild ecstasy of release washing over me. Let me know the sensation of your soaked knickers clinging to my hardening fly. Let me memorize the charismatic, fluid texture of your warm piss as it creeps saucily between your clenching thighs and my bony hips. Come wet me, darling.

Driving toward Daniel's building, Kara wondered if she was the only woman on earth who wrote flowery but crazy-lewd love letters to herself in her head—in the voice of a refined, imaginary man who lived to watch her urinate. Though the topic of her fantasies might have caused many jaws to drop, it was the voice rather than the content that puzzled Kara herself. Where the hell did that vaguely old-fashioned, literary tone even come from? English One-Fucking-Ten, way back in freshman year?

But she recognized that she wanted, someday, to have a man like that—a man whose soft, soothing voice would fuck her with its eloquence. A man who would convince her, with earfuls of beautiful words, that the sight of Kara Rebecca Wallace taking a leak was positively sublime. That's why the fantasies were so powerful, she realized. They represented exactly what she craved. She wanted to be someone's pissing paragon of loveliness. *Paragon*—now there, thought Kara, was a nice leftover word from college. She wished she remembered more words like that.

With aching reluctance, she resolved to put her fantasies aside for the moment, lest she end up losing it—and seducing the seat of her car with her fresh piss, rather than Daniel.

Right where the street skirted the park, she hit a red light. She looked around at the scenery while her knees twitched together, and she saw a young man lying on his back along a thick stone wall. His girlfriend stood above him, her feet positioned on either side of his waist. Her knees were bent enough to allow her to reach down and clasp both his hands. Kara noticed that the young woman was weaving gently from side to side, as if she were peeing lovingly onto her boyfriend. She realized that she was projecting her own obsessions, that this was almost certainly not what was happening; but, symbolically, the feeling Kara got from the scene was of that kind of intimacy, that kind of tender anointment (as the voice in her head might say). Her hand fluttered down from the steering wheel and pressed tightly against her underwear.

The green light snapped her out of it. So much for keeping her mind off her favorite topics. She was still managing not to dribble pee into her panties, but they were getting damp enough that it almost didn't matter. With a laugh, she acknowledged that, however you sliced it, Kara R. Wallace was all about wet panties this afternoon.

A few minutes later, she had parked her car and was heading up the stairs of a nondescript downtown office building. Daniel, who wrote content for various local websites and dabbled in tech support, inhabited a tiny space—a desk, a filing cabinet, a phone, a bathroom. He'd be alone there, as always, and it would be the perfect setting.

She walked through the office door, ready to make a big splash for...

A man she'd never seen before?

"Oh, hi," Kara said, at a loss, her crotch pulsating with all kinds of insistence. "I was looking for Daniel."

"I think he'll be out the rest of the day," said the stranger. "He had a meeting with a client. I'm just here to work on his quarterly taxes till I take off at five." The man instinctively looked at his watch.

Ah, Kara thought. *The occasional accountant needed by every small business.*

But she had not come here to piss herself for an occasional accountant.

"Gotcha," she said. "Do you mind if I use the restroom before I leave?"

Sitting on the toilet, she almost felt like crying. This pee should have been for *him,* damn it. But she quickly saw that a sulky, defeatist attitude was stupid—and unnecessary. There would always be more pee. It was her birthright.

Let me watch you in the morning, when you tiptoe into your bathroom, only to eschew the seat awhile. Let me enjoy the sight of you brushing your teeth or combing your hair, while your body twists and shimmies in a manner that I know feels as delectable to you as it looks to me. Let me see you wriggle as you sit on the bed, pulling up your beige stockings. Let me silently observe you as you stand jiggling before the dresser, slowly donning bra, blouse…even earrings. Allow me to study you while you study yourself in the full-length mirror, so satisfied with the lascivious elegance of your bare-bottom, bare-cunt ensemble. You are dressed everywhere, delicious woman, except across your intimate turf. Permit me to follow you as you walk back to the bathroom, which you do as if you were crossing the lobby of some stately building. You have confident, busi-nesslike strides, as though your readiness to pee were your most discreetly kept secret. Then spread your legs, like a sex-hungry lover, and I will watch you lower your naked ass onto the seat, to finally give yourself over to the sea that rises within.

Even with her bladder empty, the fantasies made her squirm. As she switched the engine off in her driveway, one hand was already active inside her moist panties.

She had the rest of the day free, and she had a pretty good idea of what she was going to do with it.

Come drink wine with me, and let loose your brazen torrents in my bathroom, your breath ripe with a tipsy vitality. Then we shall continue to drink together, until, at last, you release yourself over me. Yes, I long to share tangibly in your sensuality, to come alive with erotic fever beneath a private rainstorm of urgent, splashing fluid from your dancing body. Teach my hands to tickle at your nipples and surprise you under your arms, while you soak my loins with the poetry of your urination, my special one.

As horny as she was, Kara giggled at these fanciful words—words of her own creation. But hey, she thought, why the hell shouldn't she be poetry in motion, pissing down magic for the right observer?

I will visit you on your quiet nights, when you drink a pot of tea and curl up in smooth pajamas, when you read from a handwritten journal of your own erotic whispers until you can't sit still. Those nights upon which you escort yourself into an empty bathtub, ensconced all the while in your sleek silk. Those nights you clutch your knees and play private films in your head…until you're luxuriating, from throbbing pussy to delicate asscheeks, in your own warm puddle.

Lying on her bed and petting herself between orgasms, she remembered how it had all started. The college party at which the guy she'd been hot for all semester had shown up—on the arm of one of her friends. She recalled, in her mind and in her panties, how she'd become so excited, watching from across the room as he nibbled her friend's ear and stroked her friend's ass, that she had literally wet her pants. And how fiercely it had turned her on to feel herself losing control between her legs, under such sexy circumstances.

Kneel and dance above my face, holding your water precisely as long as you like, mesmerizing me with your gyrations, inviting me to lick you from moist to uncontrollably wet. Let me bring your source to my lips, to communicate and commune with the powerful river that flows from between your soft legs.

Her mind raced while her fingers worked in her panties. Finally, even the seductive voice in her head was drowned out by her shrieks.

Following an afternoon of slow- and fast-cooking masturbation, Kara showered and dressed for a friendly dinner with Daniel—which she knew it would be premature to describe as a date. But despite the sexually noncommittal stance that Daniel had taken thus far, Kara had high hopes. She felt sure that he was the type who would stare transfixed, rather than turning away, when she stood before him and suddenly, studiously, watered her panties, looking him in the eye so there could be no mistaking the deliberateness of her act.

How you like being dressed to the nines, my vixen—heels, stockings, skirt, blazer, and blouse—but pussy and upper thigh in the raw, crouching over me and slowly pissing, pissing, pissing. Pissing freely, then stopping abruptly, to dwell in a no-man's-land where the pleasure of letting go and the pleasure of holding it in can coexist...only to let go again when the moment calls for it, dribbling lazily over me while time stands still. A woman's time is her own while she pees; the world will wait for you, my flower. How rapt you hold me each time you hesitate, as I watch you relishing your moistened wriggles, each so pregnant with anticipation. Then, each time you resume, you once again have me writhing in masculine ecstasy beneath your feminine faucet.

She made a mental note to drink plenty of wine, and plenty of water, at the restaurant. If she could just get him back to his place, or her place, with a full bladder rocking inside her body...

Tonight, lovely one, I have your water upon my flesh before, during, and after our sensuous fucking. Before—when you're so eager to have me that you're subtly leaking, and I stroke your knickers just where you drip preciously down; when you piss hurriedly, impatiently over my caressing hand and into the bowl, taking care not to empty entirely. Then, during—as we fuck upon a dark, luscious towel, knowing that you've saved some, so that when I make you come hard enough, you will bathe me. And after—when I hold your chest close against my waist while you empty at last into the commode, your liquid kissing my fingertips, the fluorescent light humming to our heartbeats while the orgasmic kineticism of your act pulses through you. I feel you relax, by stages, in my arms, and your body becomes heavy with a grand, sensual contentment. And yet the flow has barely stopped when I feel the relaxation across your pussy begin to blossom into fresh arousal.

Daniel was late for dinner, and Kara decided to get a head start on the wine and the water. She sipped the two in alternation, enjoying the music that was piped in over the restaurant's speakers...and wondering where he was.

He was sincerely apologetic when he phoned her, fifteen minutes after he should have been there. He explained that he'd been stuck in a monster traffic jam, with no reception. And that when he'd finally been able to connect, he'd found a frantic message from a client whose computer had crashed—one hour before vital spreadsheets were due on the desks of some bigwigs. He bowed out of dinner but suggested she call him in a little while. Maybe they could catch a movie.

After her solitary dinner, Kara profited from the summer eve sunlight to take a leisurely stroll around the immediate neighborhood— a quiet section of the city. As she did so, she began to feel the effects of the wine and water she had diligently consumed.

This wasn't one of those times when it came over her suddenly and made her rush for a bathroom. No, she recognized it as one of the slower-building needs, when the reservoir would inch gradually upward over the course of an hour or so. This was something to be savored, as she would savor the sensation of ice cream melting reluctantly against her tongue. She continued her stroll, nurturing the sweet, arousing ache in her groin. The scents of countless trees wafted through the air, and even that felt arousing to her.

Lying in your room with my eyes closed, I hear you bounce lightly out of bed. I doze off to the distant, charming music of your waters, as your stream cascades merrily into the porcelain.

As the voice resonated from her mind to her pussy, Kara was surprised to find that she had miscalculated, and that she really had to pee now. Perhaps, she belatedly realized, it was because she had failed to account for the accelerating effect of being so aroused.

She could scurry back to the restaurant and apologetically avail herself of their facilities. Or she could hustle to her car and head for a nearby supermarket, convenience store, or fast-food joint. And yet…she was by herself on a secluded, residential block. Her eyes widened and her clit tingled when she realized she had an excuse to do something she'd always wanted to do.

Twice today, she had been cheated out of wetting her panties for Daniel. The least she could do for herself, Kara reasoned, was grab the consolation prize of peeing on the sidewalk. Her hands began to tremble with excitement.

There was a specific way she needed to do this, as it had been rehearsed in her mind countless times. Her panties came off. All the way off.

She closed her eyes as she began, and she let the gentle voice in her mind describe what he would have seen:

How beautiful you look in the evening light, panty-free, making your personal puddle on this deserted stretch of walkway. Let me admire you face-on as you stand spread-eagled, your skirt hiked to your waist and held in place by your cheeky elbows. My eyes are drawn to your dainty fingers, which pry your private lips apart while you sway softly into your business. Let me walk around you and stare unblinkingly as you descend into a feminine squat, your summer-sweet ass hovering proudly above the darkening pavement.

As the sun began to set, she walked jauntily back to the restaurant parking lot, a woman who had just pissed on the sidewalk and wouldn't have missed it for the world.

Sitting in her car, nude and damp under her skirt, she fingered her slick lips with one hand while dialing Daniel with the other.

Does the dampness excite you, knowing that what's tickling your thighs is the remnant of the fountain you poured onto public cement? While you wiggle in your car, do you feel the clinging wetness merging with fresh, fragrant juice from your fruit?

Her orgasm arrived before the second ring. Daniel picked up on the third.

She told him she was tired, and suggested they call it a night. They arranged to have dinner the following Friday. That was what she wanted, Kara affirmed to herself as she hung up. To wet herself for Daniel some other time. Because tonight, she was not to be the seducer, but the seduced. Tonight, she had a date at home with a very articulate voice in her head.

She took a large gulp from her water bottle and started the engine.

LEARNING HER LESSON

KELLY WALKED INTO CLIFF'S ROOM and almost had an orgasm. Or at least, that's how she remembered it later. She was in college, a perky junior with the body of a cheerleader and the dirty mind of a stripper. By day, she was a chemistry major, huddled over lab work that would make a lesser student balk, but she was diligent, never missing a class, going to office hours, probing her experiments and poring over her studies almost religiously. Because she was so intensely focused on her schoolwork, she didn't have much time for traditional dating, and besides, the guys she met at school simply seemed lacking. It was all about football, beer, and scoring, and on the few occasions she allowed them the latter, they didn't seem to know what to do with her body aside from groan, thrust, and come.

She found her fantasies turning increasingly kinky, increasingly dirty, and increasingly hot. When she woke up for the third time that week with her hands above her head, her body poised in a position of pure submission, ass in the air, the image of her getting her butt spanked good and hard still filling her mind, she knew it was time to do something about it. She was a smart cookie, and applied her usual rigor to finding just the right guy to deflower her ass. She didn't want there to be any confusion on the matter; didn't want him to treat her too delicately, or assume she was signing on to be his full-time slave. She wanted an expert, a man who truly knew his way around a woman's bottom, knew how to make it sing and soar and sting and blossom.

In her diligent research, she'd sought out those she'd heard went to dungeons and sex parties, including the girl who'd written an entire column in the school paper about how she liked to get tied up. They were more than happy to talk, amusement lurking in their features as Kelly took out her pen and notepad, scribbling things like *safeword* and *consent* and *totally fucking hot* between the ruled lines. She kept her professional face on, a mask of pleasant interest that was so far removed from the way she jerked off wildly later that her interviewees would've been shocked, or so she thought. But Kelly was good at leading a double life, or at least keeping her true self under wraps. She knew she'd never be like these outspoken, brazen scenesters, strutting their love for beatings and submission all across town. She liked being the good girl and, in fact, she was the good girl, through and through; she just knew, with increasing fervor, that she needed to surrender every once in a while, to play at being a bad girl with someone who'd properly reward her for it.

All her subjects told her that if she really wanted to find out more, she should contact Cliff. Just "Cliff," no last name; he didn't need one.

He'd graduated a few years ago and worked from home creating video games and computer programs and performing other technical tasks that were beyond her comprehension. She didn't really care about that, anyway; she barely even asked what he looked like. The girls had such glowing praise, their excitement was catching. She was entranced by the way their eyes had lit up, every last one who told her about Cliff. "He's just such a natural top." "He's incredible." "I never wanted to leave," said one particularly punky, tough-looking girl, her spiky hair, holes in her ears and visible nipple piercings giving way to a look of tenderness when she spoke about Cliff.

Nothing came up about him online, so Kelly didn't have any photos to fuel her fantasies, but that didn't stop her from turning off all the lights, lying facedown and naked, and slipping her hands between her legs as she pictured this mysterious, kinky Cliff beating her ass something fierce. She pictured him climbing on top of her, pinning her down, telling her he knew how big a slut she really was. Before she'd even met him, she was ready to give him whatever he wanted if he'd make even a fraction of her fantasies come true.

It wasn't exactly easy getting in touch with him; the girls were happy to regale her with stories, but getting his contact information was a bit trickier. Kelly suspected that despite her efforts to disguise her very personal interest in the topic, once she probed further, asking details about his methods, they could read her naughty intentions beneath her professional poise and they knew just how wet the idea of submitting to Cliff was making her. But finally Donna, who Kelly had pestered several times, took pity on her. "But don't go to his place unless you're ready to offer yourself to him one hundred percent," she said. Her words could have been ominous but to Kelly they were musical, magical. She didn't know precisely what they meant, but she wanted to find out as soon as possible.

Cliff didn't exactly sound thrilled by her call. "What do you want?" he growled, his voice deep but not in the sexy way she'd imagined.

"Well, um, Donna gave me your number and I'm doing a story on kink on campus and I wanted to see if I could interview you," she blurted, using the lie she'd given to all the other people she'd talked to. Though she didn't really consider it a lie, because if all went well, she would fashion her personal research into something worthy of a news story.

"I don't give interviews, sorry."

"Well, this could be off the record. I do have a…personal interest in the topic. A curiosity, if you will."

"If it's personal, I could fit you in. And by that I mean, if you think you have what it takes to submit to me, to surrender that professional poise you've got down and let me show you something truly new. I especially like virgins," he said. Kelly wasn't technically a virgin, but at this new game, she certainly felt like one. "Is there something else you want, Kelly?" he asked, the way he said her name sending shivers along her neck even through the phone.

It was his way of flirting, but his voice was still flat. She knew this was her one chance to get what she most desperately craved. "Yes, there is." She paused, not sure how to phrase it. "I've never done anything kinky in my life but now it's all I can think about. I want to be tied up, gagged, spanked, beaten. All of it." She was mortified that she'd lost control like that, let it spew out so quickly rather than doing a slow reveal.

Kelly was rewarded with a laugh from the other end of the phone. "You just made my cock hard, Kelly, so that means I'm going to let you come over. I only top girls who turn me on, girls I want to fuck, and I won't know that until I see you. So you should really get your ass over here right now." He gave her the address, which was only a mile away. "Wear a short skirt, and don't wear panties. And be ready for what you asked for and more. I'm not gonna go easy on you, little girl. And nobody will be around to hear you scream."

If his words were intended to scare her, they did the exact opposite. "Yes, Sir," she said, the three-letter final word sounding foreign coming from her lips, yet totally natural in her own way. She was dripping wet and wanted to jerk off but knew that if she didn't race over there, Cliff might be gone. He hung up without saying anything further.

She stripped completely, taking a moment to peek at her large breasts, the nipples already hard, the flat stomach giving way to her lightly fuzzed pussy, freckles dotting her legs, her short red hair seeming brighter in the mirror than usual. Naked, she looked cute, a word she'd always gotten flung her way, rather than the desired beautiful, or even pretty. She hoped Cliff thought she was beautiful, worthy.

Kelly found a very short tennis skirt, the white pleats beaming an innocence she knew she didn't possess. She also knew the curves of her tight ass were almost visible beneath it as she slipped on flip-flops and grabbed a white tank top, not bothering with a bra. She hurried out the door after a swipe of lip-gloss and one quick glance in the mirror. Kelly held her head high as she walked rapidly across town, ignoring the whistles from boys on bikes or leaning out of car windows.

None of them knew how to give her what she really wanted, she was sure. She wanted it hard, she wanted it to hurt.

As she rang the doorbell at a small white house, she smiled to herself. It looked like someplace she'd go to babysit, not get tied up. She fidgeted, feeling her wet, swollen pussy lips between her legs. The door opened and there was Cliff. He pulled her roughly inside, not bothering with a hello, then shut the door and dragged her down a hallway to his room. It happened so fast she barely had time to look around or take in anything more than the fact that he was over a foot taller than her, but when she saw what hung on his walls, her whole body went cold, then hot. Hanging from hooks were knives, handcuffs, paddles, and floggers. It looked like a sex toy store, and it was almost too much for her to take in. Almost, but not quite. He turned to stare at her, assessing her body. "Turn around and lift up your skirt, Kelly. I want to make sure you can follow instructions."

She liked that he jumped right into their play, not letting her pause to question it. Her body was humming in a way it never had with any of the guys she'd fucked. She'd enjoyed herself with them, but she'd never felt like her pussy was literally dripping, never felt like she had found exactly what she'd been craving. She turned away from him, bent slightly at the waist, and lifted her skirt. She'd recently shaved her pussy, and knew he could see that as well as her buttcheeks. "Very good," he said, then walked toward her. Before Kelly knew what was happening, he was slicing the tank top with a pair of scissors, then ripping the rest with his bare hands.

She whimpered. "You won't be needing this but I might," he said. She just nodded, already too aroused to properly speak. He turned her around so she was facing him, staring into her eyes. She figured she probably looked a little scared, which she was, but she was even more aroused, standing there in just her skirt and flip-flops. She got a good look at his face. He had a short brown beard and a thick head of hair, and big brown eyes that seemed to swallow her. He reached down and pinched one nipple, then tugged her forward with it. The pressure kept getting more intense, but he didn't say anything to acknowledge what he was doing. She chanced to look down, watching as he twisted her nipple between his fingers. Seeing him do it made her gasp, and he tugged on the other, pressing each nub as flat as he could between his fingers. It was starting to really hurt, but the harder he did it, the more Kelly wanted to see how much she could take.

"Yeah," he said softly as he took things up a notch, pulling and twisting at the same time. She began to pant, quick outbursts of breath that helped her deal with the pain. She felt a trickle of wetness running down her leg. When he finally let go, even though she was relieved, she wished he'd kept doing it. "Put your hands behind your back, and keep them there," he said. She was still facing him, her nipples recovering from the brief torture session.

"You wanted more, didn't you, Kelly? You're not as innocent as you look, are you?" he asked, pinching her cheek with all the roughness he'd used on her nipple. That hurt, too, but in a different way, like he was trying to let her know that he was in control of every part of her body and could touch her any way he wanted to.

"Yes, Cliff," she said, then moaned when she was rewarded with a smack across her left breast. His free hand clutched her short hair, barely able to grasp her there, while he moved so that he was perpendicular to her, then hit her breast head-on. Cliff pulled Kelly's head back and then struck her other breast. This was something she hadn't thought about beforehand, hadn't imagined anyone doing, but she liked it. A lot. She liked the way his strokes hit her nipples but also the rest of each breast. He alternated those big, open-handed smacks with flicks of his middle finger against her nubs, a constant barrage of pain that seemed to blend into heat and pleasure almost immediately.

She'd begun breathing through her nose—deep, shuddering breaths, her eyes closed—while Cliff spanked her breasts. She'd have laughed if someone had told her a year ago she'd be submitting to this, and laughed even harder at the idea that it was making her unbearably wet. She finally opened her eyes, staring up at his wall of kink, just before the last blow landed. Kelly looked down at her breasts only to find her normally pale, milky skin adorned with flashes of red, a few spots of purple. She furrowed her brow, looking up at him with shock as she realized she wanted even more. Kelly didn't know how to say it, exactly, but when Cliff leaned down and sucked each nipple between his teeth, slapping his tongue against one while pinching the other, then switching, she knew he understood.

"Lift up your skirt for me," he said after a few minutes of suckling. He knelt on the ground in front of her, his back against his bed, while Kelly stood there, feeling red rise to her cheeks. It was one thing for him to spank her, even her breasts, but to stare like that, so close-up, at her shaved pussy, made her burn. "Now put your hand here," he said, indicating the area just above her clit. "Pull it tight." She didn't question his orders, didn't question anything that was happening because every word from his lips was music to her cunt. She pulled, feeling the stretch of her skin down there just as she felt the corresponding ache deep inside. That's when he spanked her. There. Right on her pussy lips. Hard. Kelly was holding her skirt up with one hand and her cunt tight with the other, and she wished she had something to lean on.

The smacks kept coming, right on her most sensitive area. They hurt, but the moment they were done she found herself wanting more of them, liking that she could take that kind of intensity. She wanted his fingers to shift a little, go inside, fuck her after he'd smacked her, but Cliff didn't do that. "How old are you, Kelly?" he asked her, instead.

"Twenty-one," she answered automatically, telling the truth without thinking about the consequences.

"A fine age. You're going to count that high for me while I spank you," he said, moving her around so she was bent over a chair that was flush against his bed. Her arms lay across the mattress, while the head of the chair pressed against her lower belly. He pulled her pussy lips apart, pinching her labia for a moment before letting go. "I'll even give you a choice. I'll spank your ass or your pussy. Which will it be, Kelly?" She moaned, totally unsure which to pick. She hadn't really planned for this, even though she thought she had. She thought she'd done her research; she'd read and talked and fantasized plenty. But the reality of Cliff's hands on her, his voice drilling through her in the small room, him looming over her like this, was infinitely more exciting than anything she could've envisioned.

"My ass," she finally said, wanting to see how that would feel.

"Good choice," he said. "But since you took those smacks to your pussy so well, I'm going to have to use this paddle on you. I'll let you look at it first." He took a rounded black paddle off the wall. It looked like a Ping-Pong paddle to her, but was coated with black leather. He held it in front of her face, then closer. "Kiss it," Cliff said, tapping it against her lips, which she dutifully pursed. "You have a very beautiful ass," Cliff told her.

She wasn't expecting a compliment, and beamed as if he'd told her she'd won the school talent show. "But wait, I think I need to cuff your wrists first. You look like you might just try to move and escape, or fidget just enough to throw me off." Kelly moaned as he reached over to the far side of the wall for a pair of padded handcuffs that he proceeded to fasten around her wrists. She watched as he bound her, just as she'd dreamed about, and felt her body sink into the sweet bliss of immobilization when he was done. She kept testing the cuffs, not to see if she could escape, but to ensure that she couldn't. Now she really was his, her ass front and center, ready for him. As if reading her mind, he said, "Those pretty cheeks are going to be even more beautiful when I'm done with them. I want you to count, and start with, 'One, thank you, Cliff.' If you miss one, we'll have to start over."

"Okay," she said, sure she could follow this simple rule twenty-one times. The first blow sent her body digging into the chair, the slap ringing through the room. The paddle was harsh, stinging her skin, but she focused not on the pain, but the counting. Whereas before Kelly had been absorbing every aspect of his smacks to try to fully recreate them later in her journal, now she had to focus on spitting out those four words, rapid-fire, because his blows were coming one after the other. "Thirteen, thank you, Cliff," she said breathlessly, rewarded instantly with another hard smack landing equally upon both ass-cheeks. The next made her ass jiggle in a way that shook her cunt, too. She heard the paddle whiz through the air, the sound one that was only audible if the room was completely still and quiet, and she flinched when it landed on the bed next to her. Cliff put his hand on the small of her back, right above her tailbone, then beat out the final seven blows.

Kelly surprised herself by not missing the count at all. When he stepped away, her ass was hot, hurting even more, seemingly, than it had while he was doing it. Cliff stared down at her. "Well, Kelly, you've been very good. I think this should give you something to think about when you get home." He untied her and tossed the torn tank top back at her. "I didn't have to gag you with this; maybe next time I'll get some screams out of you that will necessitate shutting those pretty lips." He spoke like she was almost not even there, as if he could plan everything out without her cooperation, and she liked that. For some reason, she knew that if she truly objected, he'd stop whatever he was doing in an instant. Knowing this not only turned her on, but made her long to sink deeper into his debt, offer herself up more fully next time. She glanced down and saw his erection bulging in his pants.

She wanted to ask about it, wanted to ask why he wasn't shoving her down to the ground and making her suck it, or making her bend over again and slamming it into her pussy. She'd have gladly done either one, and in fact, both her mouth and cunt pouted in arousal. "You want this, don't you, Kelly?" he asked, taking her hand and placing it on his hardness.

She nodded, gripping his erection tightly between her fingers as she held the tatters of her shirt in her hand. Now she really wanted it.

"Too bad. One of the first things you need to learn in the kinky world is that you can't always get what you want. And sometimes it's good for you not to. Sometimes it's good for you to go home with a wet pussy and some marks on you," he said, tracing the bruises on her chest while running his fingers along her slit.

"You have to work your way up to having my cock. Maybe if you come over again I'll let you watch me fuck a girl who's earned that privilege. You can watch me bend her over and fuck her so hard she cries." Now all Kelly wanted was to touch herself. She was practically ready to come right then thinking about what Cliff had just described.

"I want you to wait one week, and if you're still wet like this, you can call me, and maybe we can have another lesson. I want to make sure you have enough time to think about what you're doing." Again she nodded, mesmerized by his mastery. "Oh, and Kelly? No touching yourself until you call. If I want you to come, I'll either make it happen myself or I'll tell you it's okay. This way I'll find out just how devoted you are to me, how close you are to deserving some of this," he said, whipping out his cock. He wrapped his fist around it and stroked it slowly, making her quiver.

"Now if you'll excuse me," he said, steering her toward the door even though she had just the torn shirt to cover her reddened breasts and nothing to hide her very wet cunt from any breezes that might hike up her skirt. She scrambled to put the shirt on over her head, her body coming down slightly off its high. He practically shoved her out the door and she walked home in a daze, hardly noticing the stares and catcalls, her ears filled with the sounds of his smacks, his voice.

Kelly was surprised to see that only two hours had passed since she'd left. It felt like days. She lay down on her bed, on her stomach, her hands above her head. The position was familiar, yet totally new, and her body was burning in places she had never expected it to.

It's going to be a long week, she thought, smiling into her pillow as she spread her legs and dreamed of Cliff.

TSAURAH LITZKY

MY FAVORITE UNCLE

K ING OF THE TENOR SAXOPHONE" was how my favorite Uncle
Irving was known during his long and illustrious career. He was
world famous and worked with all the great old-time dance bands.
Not really my uncle, he was my father's best friend. Now he is over
eighty, and I'm the only family he's got.

For the past few years he has been confined to a wheelchair and
living in the Home for Aged and Indigent Gentlemen Musicians in
Sayreville, Long Island. Once a month, I ride out to visit him on the
Long Island Railroad. I always bring him a bottle of Canadian Club
secreted at the bottom of a big bag of popcorn because liquor is for-
bidden inside the home. If I have had a new erotic story anthologized,
I bring him one of my author's copies. Uncle Irv loves my stories. He
says that since there are no women residents in the home and the
nurses are foolishly impervious to his charms, my stories are all the sex

he gets. This time I do have a new book for him; a collection titled *Kinks and Winks* just out from Make Nice Press.

It's a beautiful summer day. I walk the few blocks from the station to the home in what was once a fine old Victorian mansion. I'm glad Uncle is spending his old age in such a serene setting.

The common room isn't crowded. A few ancients are playing cards at a table near the door. Uncle Irving is seated in his wheelchair next to a big armchair. His smile when he sees me is huge. He is completely bald and is wearing an immaculate white shirt and one of the bow ties from his giant collection. Today it is a peach one with purple polka dots, maybe because he knows peach is my favorite color.

"Hi, Trixie," my uncle greets me. He often calls me Trixie, after his longtime girlfriend, Trixie Coyle, now deceased nine years. She was a showgirl he met at the Copacabana. Sometimes I think Uncle may even think I am Trixie, because suddenly while we are talking he will put his hand above my knee on my thigh and leave it there. I don't mind.

"You look so pretty," Uncle says, "like a daffodil in that yellow dress. How is my niece, the famous writer?"

"I'm not famous yet," I say. I kiss him on his shiny pate and sit down in the armchair.

"You will be famous if you keep writing those naughty stories. Did you bring me one today? Did you bring me my popcorn?"

"Absolutely," I tell him. "Your popcorn is right here and I also have a new book." I open my tote bag and pull out *Kinks and Winks*.

"What's with this kinks?" Uncle Irving wants to know. "Kinky is hair, all frizzy, snarled up like steel wool." I tell him that's true, "But," I continue, "kink is also what you do when you play let's pretend while you are doing it. It's a way of making it especially hot. You can use costumes and stuff, you and your partner make it into a play or a wacky game."

He looks pensive, then he says, "You mean like when the husband wants the wife to wear high heels to bed or if I tied one of the nurses to the toilet in the bathroom with bandages and then had my way with her? I've always had a thing for nurses."

"Correct," I answer.

"I see," he says and he opens *Kinks and Winks* and flips to the index. "Here's your story, 'Triangle Titillation.' What's that one about?" I tell him it's about a fictional me doing the horizontal mambo with a boyfriend and the boyfriend's best friend. "Fictional?" says my uncle, raising an eyebrow. I tell him I only wish such a thing would happen. "You are so naughty," he teases me.

" 'Yellow Rain over Babbling Brook' by Rod Rushing; what kind of a kink is this?" he wants to know.

"If you think about the title, you will probably know," I answer. A blush spreads from the top of his head all the way down to the collar of his shirt.

"People are now writing about these things, things that used to be such big secrets no one would dream of talking about them," Uncle says.

"Sure, this is the twenty-first century, the third millennium," I tell him. "It's a new world."

Uncle starts to laugh. "Ha, I was a kinkster, already. I didn't know there was a name for it."

"You old devil! What were you and Trixie up to?"

"I'll tell you," he says, "only it wasn't Trixie. Come, let's go to my room." I know this means he wants us to have our usual cocktail. He wheels himself ahead of me out of the common room and down the long hall to his corner room with the four big windows. The walls are covered with pictures, photos of Trixie, the bands he played with, long dead cousins and uncles and aunts.

Uncle rolls over to the little table next to the bureau. I get the whiskey glasses from the hiding place beneath the socks in his underwear drawer. I sit down beside him in the only chair, extract the Canadian Club from the bag of popcorn in my backpack. I pour us each a solid shot. We click glasses and drink the liquor down. "Delicious," says Uncle. "This whiskey has no regrets."

"Now," I say, "tell me about your kink. Why wasn't Trixie your kink partner?"

"This was before I even knew Trixie. Back when we were playing the Tutti-Frutti Club in Manhattan, we had a torch singer with the band. Her name was Lucy Loose. She was huge, the guys in the band used to joke about her. *Here comes Lucy Loose, big in the front, bigger in the caboose.* She had wild black hair. I liked to watch her shake her thing while she was doing her numbers. I began to wonder since she had so much hair on her head did she have so much on her...you know. One night I asked her to have a drink with me when the show was over. After a few martinis at the club bar, I asked her the big question.

" 'Miss Lucy, you have such beautiful, thick hair on your head, I can't stop myself from being curious. Do you have so much hair on your, um...secret place?'

"It took a moment before she answered, it not being a usual question and all. She looked down into her glass, then right back up at me, straight into my eyes. 'Why, yes, Irv,' she answered with a grin on her face. 'Yes, I do.'

"That was when I knew I was in. It took one more martini before I asked her if she liked to play dress-up games. She said yes again. She quickly agreed when I suggested I rent a room at the St. Damian Hotel for next Sunday night when the band had off. I would bring the costume.

"I went to a uniform store and purchased a nurse's uniform, an extra-large. I reserved a room and told Lucy the room number after our show Saturday night. We were to meet at eight the following evening. You can bet I was there an hour early. I put the lights on dim, put 'Some Enchanted Evening' on the record player and ordered a bottle of the best champagne to be sent up from room service. Besides the big double bed, there was a nice couch in the room. I had the bell-hop put the champagne on the coffee table in front of the couch. I tipped him twenty for good luck. I got the nurse's outfit from the bag it was in and set it out neatly on the bed. I sat on the couch waiting for Lucy.

"Finally, there was a knock on the door. I was nervous and my heart was pounding like a kettledrum.

"There was Lucy, towering over me like a giantess. She was wearing a red dress cut so low I could see the top of her nipples. Her magnificent breasts, held high by some kind of intricate corset, just cleared my head. I stood there gaping. Finally she says, 'Irv, aren't you going to invite a lady in and offer her a drink?'

" 'Sure, sure,' I say and I beckon her in and lead her to sit down on the sofa. When she sees the nurse's outfit, she starts to giggle. 'Oh, are we going to play doctor?' she wants to know. 'Not exactly,' I tell her.

"Pretty soon we are sipping bubbly. It turns out that Miss Lucy loves champagne and it's not long before I got one of my hands inside her décolletage and she has my other hand up to her mouth. She is sucking my fingers, running her nice pink tongue between them, and from the way Lucy is shifting her hips from side to side I'm thinking maybe she is ready to play. I ask her, 'Lovely Lucy, are you ready to play a dress-up game?'

" 'I'm ready to do whatever you want to do,' she says.

"I say, 'Now, I want you to take the nurse's uniform into the lava-tory, get out of your dress and put on the uniform.' 'Will do,' she says. 'I always looked good in white.' Then I ask her, 'Are you wearing a garter belt to show off those fine black silk stockings you have on?'

" 'Yes,' Lucy answers, 'I'm wearing a pretty pink garter belt with the cutest little red bows.' I tell her to take off her knickers but leave the garter belt and stockings on and also I ask her to leave on the red sling-back high heel pumps she is wearing. I tell her they accent her gorgeous gams and shapely ankles. 'You sure know how to make a lady feel like a million bucks,' she says as she rises from the couch. She shuts the door of the loo behind her. I whisk off all my clothes, including my shoes and socks. I go sit on the bed.

"When she comes out, she stands directly in front of me so my head is level with her crotch. With trembling fingers I start to undo the buttons down the front of the nurse's uniform from the bottom up; one, two, three, four, five buttons right up to the waist. I pull open the uniform and there, framed by the pink lace of the garters and those cute red bows, is the biggest, glossiest, curliest most beautiful black bush I could imagine. Lucy puts her hands on my shoulders, starts to gently massage the back of my neck.

" 'Come to mama,' she says and I wonder if she's played this game before.

"I lower my face into her verdant garden. I take some of that hair into my mouth, between my teeth. I tug gently then move south, nuzzling her delta. I am suffused by her aroma, a combination of Ivory soap, some expensive perfume, maybe Chanel No. 5, and something else, an underlying odor salty like the sea. I send out my tongue, my advance scout. I soon find what I'm looking for, her shy bud, her little cockette. I begin to kiss, nibble, tongue it. I suck on it until it swells to the size of a grape."

I was so engrossed in the story. I hadn't realized my hand was all curled up in my skirt, on top of my vulva, pressing against it. Uncle Irv didn't seem to notice. He was looking up, over my head. "I was in paradise," Uncle went on. "Lucy was still rubbing my neck. I was sucking her like a hero and my fingers were around that fellow between my legs. I was close to bringing myself off when Lucy pipes up, 'Irv, you bad, bad boy, you bit me!' If I did, I certainly didn't realize it. I stopped doing what I was doing between Lucy's legs. 'I'm so sorry,' I said, 'I never wanted to hurt you, Lucy dear.'

" 'Sorry' she snorted. 'Sorry or not, you are a bad, bad boy and deserve a spanking!'

"Lucy stepped back, unbuttoned the top of the nurse's uniform and let it fall to the floor. What a body, her knockers were bigger than watermelons. She sat down on the bed, grabbed me like I was a powder puff, flipped me over and slammed me on top of her knees. She held me down with one arm over my rib cage, and then she started smacking me with the palm of the other. At first it stung, making my skin tingle, but then I got to kind of like it.

"Each time her hand came down, her soft bosoms bounced like fat fluffy pillows against my back. The stick between my legs was hard as a rock, but still I could swear it was getting bigger and bigger. Then Lucy stopped and, and well, you can imagine what happened next."

"I certainly can, Uncle," I answer. "You are such a great storyteller, and," I add, "you sure are an amazing kinkster."

"Thanks, Trixie," he says. "So, are you going to write a story about me?"

"What do you think?" I ask him, and pour us another drink.

N. T. MORLEY

SIT and SPIN

K ASEY SHOWED UP for her first spinning class dressed in her brand-spanking-new workout clothes and ready for something exciting. As soon as she saw the instructor, however, she wasn't quite sure. She had heard about him from the other women at the health club. A mammoth Norwegian, he was rumored to have a lascivious streak. From the looks of the spinning machines, Kasey figured that had to be true.

There were a dozen other women scattered about, enough to almost fill the room's complement of machines. The women stretched and warmed up, bending their limber bodies into improbable positions. Kasey had already stretched.

"Let's get started," said the Norwegian with only the slightest trace of an accent. He was a muscled Adonis in a tightly fitting top and shorts that showed off the impressive bulge of his manhood. "My name is Hans. I see from the sign-up sheet that we have a new student today. Let's all say hi to Kasey."

Kasey blushed a little as the women eyed her with great interest and said, "Hi, Kasey," in one musical purr.

"Hi," said Kasey. "Glad to be here."

"Now, Kasey, what brought you to my class?" asked Hans.

Kasey blushed deeper and shifted uncomfortably, feeling the eyes of the entire classroom of women upon her.

"I heard it was different," she said.

A giggle rippled through the room, and Hans chuckled.

"That it is," said Hans. "Well, let's get started. Everybody choose a machine, and strip."

Kasey had never undressed fully in a classroom full of women before; in lap dancing class they always wore G-strings. Still, her classmates didn't show a bit of modesty; with a whir of female flesh, T-shirts, tank tops, gym shorts and tights all ended up folded neatly next to the spinning machines. Kasey nervously removed her sports halter and bicycling shorts. Now nude except for their socks and gym shoes, the women stood obediently by their chosen machines, as if at attention. Hans walked around the room slowly, smiling at each woman before inspecting her, sometimes patting her ass or stroking her belly, exploring each body with his fingers.

"Excellent definition, Miriam," said Hans to one pert redhead, who blushed and smiled as he fondled her inner thigh. "You've really been making progress."

"Thank you," Miriam said.

When Hans got to Kasey, his hand went instantly between her legs.

She whimpered as he felt her cunt, his brow furrowed in disappointment.

"You'll definitely need additional lubricant, Kasey," said Hans. "The machines in the front of the room are self-lubricating, but this one hasn't been replaced yet. Girls, are any of you wet enough to trade with Kasey?"

"I am," said Miriam perkily, and hurried over to take Kasey's machine. Kasey obediently traded with her while she stared at the upright dildo projecting from the seat of the spinning machine Miriam had abandoned. A small slit at the top had already oozed a clear, viscous lubricant over the head, making the penis-shaped device glisten in the fluorescent light. Nonetheless, Kasey eyed the dildo uncomfortably; it was several inches longer and quite a bit thicker than the other one, which Kasey had chosen for its manageable size.

"Not too big for you, is it, Kasey?" asked Hans with a wickedness to his voice. The room erupted in little titters.

Reddening, Kasey said quickly, "No. It's just right."

Hans clapped his palms together and headed to the front of the room. "Everybody mount!"

As the other women climbed onto their machines and, perching with the heads of the dildos at their entrances, easily slid themselves onto the lubricated organs, Kasey climbed onto her own, unsure of how she was going to fit such an enormous cock into her. Kasey was no dim bulb. Now she knew why spinning class was so popular here; each new girl had to undergo this initiation, taking the one machine with an improbably large member, as if to prove she could handle it.

Kasey climbed onto the machine and spread her pussy lips with her fingers, positioning her tight opening at the head of the big cock.

She winced as she sat down, feeling the enormous head stretch her in a way she'd never been stretched before. She let out a little yelp as the head popped into her, and another round of giggles went through the room. Kasey had to wriggle her body back and forth to force herself down the length of the shaft. When she finally sat atop the dildo, she could feel the head pushing into her cervix, the thick ridges near the base rubbing against her G-spot. Every movement she made brought a fresh pulse of heat to her body. She could feel her nipples stiffening with the stimulation.

If I wasn't lubricated enough before, thought Kasey, *I definitely am now.*

"All right, ladies, let's start." Hans hit a button behind the table at the front of the room. It was a curious table, Kasey noticed, looking much like a piece of exercise equipment itself—with stirrups and a cutaway for the legs, almost like a gynecological exam table. Kasey felt a thrill: so it was true what she'd heard about Hans. More than true, from the looks of it.

When Hans hit the button for the sound system, speakers began to pump rhythmic dance music while the TV monitors in the corners of the room flickered to life. The girls in the class started cycling, and with some difficulty Kasey did the same. The throbbing beat of the music was hooked to the vibrators positioned at the base of the dildos, hers now buzzing rhythmically against Kasey's clit. But, more importantly, every turn of the pedals caused the seat to push up smoothly and then cycle back down, pounding the dildo into Kasey's cunt as surely as if an exceedingly well-hung man were fucking her. It was all she could do to maintain her grip on the handlebars and stare up, slack-jawed, at the pornographic images playing on the TV screens.

She whimpered and moaned as she fucked herself. She could hear her classmates moaning softly, as well.

"Now remember to keep up a steady rhythm," said Hans as he circled the room, patting thighs, feeling bellies. "Feel those muscles work. The vibrators go to the music, but you control how fast your cock is fucking you. Pump faster if you start to get close. Kasey, how are you doing?"

Kasey stared at him, wide-eyed, moaning softly.

"Good," he said, his hand clenching around her thigh as she worked herself up and down on the rising and falling seat, not quite matching the rhythm with her own, with the result that each thrust hit her harder. "You're really working those quads," said Hans. "Good going. Kasey, you're going to do great in my class."

"Th—thank—you," she tried to say, her eyes rolling back in her head as she pedaled faster.

"All right," said Hans. "We're going uphill. Get ready to work!"

The pedals began to resist more, and Kasey urgently pushed harder, moaning, "Oh, God, oh God!" so that the rest of the room giggled. As the speed of the dildo fucking her started to slow, Kasey pedaled faster to keep it going.

Hans paused again in front of his newest student. "Kasey looks like she's close already," he said. "Now, remember what happens to the first one who comes? We've got a special prize for her. And girls—no faking!"

Kasey desperately pumped her thighs, making the dildo pound her hard as she pulsed toward orgasm. The intensity of the vibrator at her clit increased, and within moments Kasey was moaning uncontrollably, her whole naked body rocking back and forth atop the dildo as it fucked her in time with her body's own movements.

Suddenly, Miriam let out a load groan and screamed, "I'm coming, I'm coming!" at the top of her lungs. Kasey was almost too far gone to hear it, but she dimly recognized Hans's voice: "Come on, now, Miriam! You'll have to fake it better than that if you want to win!"

Miriam looked down chastised as the other girls snickered at her.

Meanwhile, Kasey was unaware of Miriam's attempt at deception. The newest member of Hans's spinning class was perched on her dildo, pinching her own nipples, throwing her head back and shuddering all over as she edged toward an intense climax. The other girls in class watched her, and Hans stood stock-still in front of her, saying "Good girl, good girl, feel the burn, work those muscles—you're doing great, Kasey…"

When she finally came, loudly, the pleasure exploded through her naked body. She shuddered and slumped forward against the handlebars, her ass raised high on the top stroke of the dildo as her feet slipped off the pedals and she hung there in midair, suported only by the dildo.

The room broke out in applause. Hans ran to the front of the room and turned off the music, and the girls stopped cycling. Hans stripped off his shirt and dropped his shorts, revealing a huge cock rendered quite hard by recent events.

"All right, girls, it looks like our new student is the winner today! Miriam, Susie, get her down from there and put her on the table. Faceup or facedown, Kasey?"

Kasey just moaned incoherently as Susie and Miriam lifted her, with some difficulty, off the machine. They carried her up to the table at the front of the room, where Kasey eyed Hans's cock with sudden interest. It was even bigger than the dildo on her machine. Surely such a mammoth thing couldn't fit inside her.

Kasey's eyes flickered up to Hans's face, admiring the finely chiseled Nordic features and the wicked smile he gave her. He winked at her as he stroked his cock up and down, and Kasey thought she saw a jealous glance from Miriam, a glance that flickered from Hans's hard cock to Kasey's lucky pussy. Kasey looked at the huge organ and decided yes, it certainly *could* fit inside her pussy, or at least she would make a rapturous attempt to find out.

"Faceup, please," she said with a moan, spreading her legs to the edges of the table as Miriam and Susie laid her across it, her ass right at the edge of the cutaway so that her pussy was quite exposed and accessible. Hans came toward her with his cock in his hand.

Kasey's cunt was wet and slick from the self-lubricating dildo, but the feel of Hans's cockhead stroking gently up and down her slit made it juice even more. He was certainly well trained himself; rather than taking her immediately, he worked his cock from her slick entrance up to her hard clit, teasing it and making her moan for his cock, begging for it with her eyes. Hans looked down at her, clearly satisfied with himself in that way that only personal trainers can be.

"Please," Kasey begged. "Fuck me!"

The sound of giggles shimmered throughout the room. Kasey suspected that every woman in here had, at some point, been on this very table, being teased by Hans. Begging for it. But Hans was in no rush. He let go of his cock and worked his hips to slide it up and down in

Kasey's slit without entering her, reaching up to place his hands on her small, high breasts and pinch her nipples as he tantalized her.

Kasey was moaning uncontrollably, her hips working hungrily and matching the strokes of Hans's cock up and down her—and when he entered her, Kasey came almost immediately, arching her back and clawing at the table, climaxing with a loud cry of ecstasy as Hans's massive cock slid deep inside her. He began to fuck her rhythmically with great, rapid thrusts of his quadriceps, pushing his cock into her so that even if she had wanted to stop coming, she couldn't have. She soared high on the orgasm—thirty seconds, forty—and then she was pressed up against him, her ass pulled forward on the table, her arms around his neck as she pressed her face to his muscled chest. Hans lifted her fully off the table and all but bounced her up and down on his cock, his hands on her ass lifting her and dropping her down, the full weight of Kasey's body ramming her down onto his thickness so that he filled her with new vigor each time. He met the downward strokes of her body with the upward strokes of his hips, and the power of his thrusts drove Kasey toward another orgasm as her classmates cheered.

When Kasey came for the third time, whoops and applause burst out all through the room. The sounds were almost drowned out by the great thunderous groan from Hans's massive chest—he was about to come.

Planting his hands firmly on her ass and digging his fingers in—in a way that made Kasey's thighs tug against her clit—Hans lifted Kasey bodily off of his cock, setting her down on her knees like a china teacup before him. Her mouth was on his cock immediately, barely able to get around the enormous head. The taste of her own pussy only made her hungrier for his come. *He just fucked me with this cock,* thought Kasey, her clit swelling anew as she realized it. *It tastes like me.* She reached down and stroked her wet slit eagerly as she sucked him, her legs spread just wide enough to allow her easy access as she fingered herself.

She suckled Hans's huge cock eagerly. Hans uttered a loud roar and thrust his hips forward, working deeper into Kasey's mouth, deep enough that she had to open wide to take it. Hans let himself go in her mouth, and her lips came glistening off of Hans's cock, not a drop of semen having been missed. Kasey offered Hans's shaft one gentle kiss, tasting her pussy once more. She slid her hand out of her cunt and licked her fingers clean as Hans watched with pleasure, and the room burst out in applause and cheers again.

"Well," said Hans, his voice trembling from his intense orgasm. "As you see, Kasey is multiorgasmic, so class could get pretty interesting from now on. Don't forget those quad exercises, ladies, and remember your Kegels!"

Kasey's classmates began to dress. She walked with some difficulty back to her machine and picked up her shorts and sports halter. Her hand went automatically around the huge dildo, still lubricated with her cunt and its own prodigious mechanical secretions. The feel of the huge thing in her hand sent a fresh shiver through her.

She turned to Hans, who had slipped on his shorts and was pulling his shirt over his head.

"I don't suppose the room's free," she said breathlessly.

"Until the next class," said Hans with a grin, "in forty-five minutes."

Moaning softly, Kasey climbed back onto the spinning machine and began to feel the burn.

COIN OPERATED

K NEEL DOWN, BABY, and do exactly what I say." She licked her lips as he dropped to his knees, then grabbed his head with both hands and moved his face up until his eyes met her own.

"Oh, baby, I'm going to play with you tonight." She purred in anticipation, and pulled his head to her breasts. She could feel his warm breath through her shirt, and his trembling excited her. Her hands held him there, letting her anticipation build, imagining the scene in her mind until her breathing grew heavy and she was rubbing her thighs together, the denim jeans making a raspy counterpoint to her deep breaths.

She pushed his head back, told him, "Stay." Reached behind her and grabbed a paper bag, fished around in it until she found the nipple clamps. They were the clover kind that just got tighter the harder you pulled, and the mere thought of how much he hated and lusted for them made her wet. "Put them on for me, baby."

His hands trembled as she stretched her leg forward and gently massaged his cock with her foot until he groaned and leaned back, all thoughts of covering his nudity forgotten. As he brought the clamp closer to the sensitive nub of flesh on his chest, she started rubbing harder. He opened the clamp and she slid her foot under him to gently massage his balls as well. The clamp embraced his nipple and his excited moans turned to a hiss of pain.

"Come on, now the other one." Her foot stopped moving, and she only started her gentle strokes again when he began to bring the clamp toward its target, stopping when he stopped, watching his face and smiling when he clamped down the nipple. The chain connecting them danced and swayed in time with his hoarse, gasping breath.

"Stand up." He stood up on unsteady feet, and she pulled him closer by his hard cock. "Tonight you're going to be my little coin-operated fuck toy. Say it."

She watched him close his eyes and lean his head back as she slowly jacked him off, moving her hand rhythmically up and down. He swallowed hard before he answered, and she thrilled at the uncertainty and fear in his voice. "Tonight, I'm going to be your coin-operated fuck toy."

She trembled a little when she heard the words, and felt a hot flush creep up from her chest into her face. There was a watch in her hand, and she fiddled with it while he stood silently. She wrapped the band of the watch around the base of his cock, cinched it tight. "This is your timer, fuck toy. Every three minutes, it'll start vibrating. That vibrating means you stop fucking. When I push the snooze button, it'll stop vibrating, and you start fucking again. I'll give you a quarter each time, since you're a coin-operated fuck toy."

Standing up, she showed him the ball gag first. Licking it lewdly, she ran her tongue around both sides, letting it shine with her spit. She sucked it into her mouth, then pulled it out by the straps and watched his eyes widen at the *pop* when it slid past her lips. "Fuck toys don't speak." He opened his mouth wide, and she slipped the red rubber sphere in and tightened the buckle. The look of his jaw, so distended and unnatural, the straps making a harsh line around his face, made her thighs tremble.

"Fuck toys don't see." She wrapped the blindfold around his head, covering his eyes.

"Fuck toys don't have hands." She could feel the reluctance in his arms as she pulled them behind his back, and rubbed herself on his leg. Even through her clothing the friction made her moan as she ground hot pussy into his thigh, and she barely forced herself to stop when the resistance went out of his arms. The handcuffs clicked around his wrists, and she got out the last item, a simple pair of earplugs.

"Remember, toy, the vibration starts, you stop. I won't tell you again, and it wouldn't do any good anyway. Because fuck toys don't hear. A fuck toy just fucks." She ran her tongue along his earlobe and giggled at the moan that escaped the ball gag. The earplugs slid in, and she slowly took her clothes off. Blind, deaf and dumb, his hands taken away, she watched him stand there, waiting for her to turn him on.

A roll of quarters became an untidy silver circle on the bed stand. She licked her lips in anticipation and felt her nipples tighten. He stood over her seat on the edge of the bed, and she found the button that started the watch. He jumped when it started; the vibrations from the watch were strong, traveling down his cock, into his balls, and back into his body clear to the base of his spine. Her hand pulled his hardness into her, and she flicked a quarter at him that bounced off his chest.

Her fingers found the snooze button on the watch, and she lay back as the vibrations stopped and he started fucking her. She closed her eyes, let her hands wander to her breasts, and enjoyed the sensation as he blindly thrust forward, pulled back, and thrust forward again.

She felt her passion building, felt his thrusts growing more frantic and uncontrolled, until the vibrations from the watch alarm traveled down his cock and into her. He shuddered to a halt, and she slipped away, watching him shake and fight to keep his hips from thrusting his cock into the open air in a desperate search for stimulation.

Her hand wandered down to her clit, and she rubbed herself gently, laughing as the vibrations made his balls tremble and tortured his cock. Another quarter hit him in the chest and she guided him back in, letting him feel her hand reach down to turn off the timer. She lingered over the button, pinching his balls and feeling him tense under her hands. Finally she turned off the watch and lay back, wrapping her legs around his waist as he frantically began fucking the instant the vibration stopped.

She let him fuck, wrapping herself around him and bouncing a quarter off his chest every time she had to turn off the timer to start his thrusting again. Her orgasms rolled over her, and his followed. By the fourth time he'd cum, the groans had turned to whimpers and she couldn't get him hard with her hand anymore. She leaned forward, and her lips wrapped around his balls, sucking gently and then licking all the way up to the head of his cock. He tried to step back, to get away from the constant stimulation and orgasms that had turned his pubic region into a throbbing, aching mass.

Her hand wrapped around the chain on the nipple clamps, and she pulled him back to her hard. She started licking again, gently teasing swirls on the head of his cock followed by long, sensuous strokes all along the length. She doubled her efforts when she heard him moan, and pulled him in closer with the nipple clamps when he tried to pull away. Her moans of pleasure were a sultry echo of his gasps of pain.

One hand pulled his head down. Her free hand pulled out an earplug, and she brought her lips in close and whispered to him. "Listen up, fuck toy. The best part of having a toy is breaking it, and I'm going to break you. I'm going to play with you until you melt, until you collapse on the floor and won't work no matter how hard I beat you. Until my little fuck toy is shriveled and useless and burning and aching. And then I'm going to fix you, all week I'm going to let my fuck toy fill up with lust until he begs me to play with him again. And then I'm going to break you all over again, and keep fixing you and breaking you until my little coin-operated fuck toy can't be fixed anymore."

She threw a quarter at him, watched it bounce off his chest and roll across the floor and then pulled him inside her and turned the watch vibration off.

She lay back and smiled at him. She saw the pain rolling across him in waves, and watched tears run out from under the blindfold and mix with the drool running around the gag, but he started fucking her. She sighed and closed her eyes, felt the warm spasms of pleasure roll over her, and wondered how long it would take her to break her new toy.

EMILY DUBBERLEY

SERIOUS CHEEK

K NOWING WHAT YOU WANT IS ONE THING. Saying it is quite another.

"Great arse!" I don't know what made me say it, but when she walked past me in the bar, her pert cheeks hypnotized me. I'm not the sort of guy who usually accosts women in bars, with cheesy chat-up lines. But I'd had a few drinks and it really was an impeccable specimen: firm, round, each cheek clearly defined in her tight skirt, making it all too easy to picture the pleasures that lay beneath and between.

I've always been an arse man and something about hers drew an instinctive reaction from me: I wanted to cup her buttocks; knead them; caress them; part them to see her fully opened up for me; slip my fingers into her wetness from behind so that I could admire the view while feeling her writhing at my touch and hearing her begging me for more. And, I have to admit, I wanted to slap those delectable cheeks, see them getting pinker as I gradually built up the pressure and hear her moan as I alternated slapping her with fingering her wet slit.

She turned to me, and smiled. I froze. Suddenly, I was embarrassed at the images in my head. I briefly panicked as if she could read my mind and see the depravity I was mentally conjuring. It was so vivid that I wouldn't have been surprised if I'd had a thought bubble over my head for everyone in the bar to see.

"You do realize that if you weren't so good looking, I'd punch you for coming up with a line like that? But, as it is, you get a chance to buy me a drink. Assuming that your conversation isn't limited to trite compliments?"

It took me a while to register what she'd said, and when I did, I felt intimidated at her confidence—but still drawn to her. And painfully aroused. Her voice was cigarette tainted, with a slight break in it, her inflection somehow suffused with an underlying giggle.

"It wasn't meant to be trite," I said. "It just slipped out. I never usually…"

"Whatever," she said, waving away my apologies. "A bottle of Budweiser, please. And I'll be watching you so don't even think of spiking it."

As I went to the bar, my movements were hampered by the insistent erection that, although it had briefly subsided when she'd turned to challenge me, had swollen back to its former glory when she spoke. Something she noticed when I returned with her drink. She just glanced at my groin then raised an eyebrow. "Thanks for the drink. So, going to top your opening line then?"

Talk about pressure. I figured the only way to deal with her was to give as good as I got.

"Yes. You don't have a great arse. It's bloody incredible."

"Have you got an entirely one-track mind? You realize I don't have to listen to this?"

"You're right. You don't. But you are."

"In the hope that first impressions were deceptive. Anyway, I can't walk away—I know you'll be ogling me. At least when I'm facing you, you can't eye me up."

"Impeccable logic. So you're going to continue talking to me, even though you find me loathsome, just so I can't look at your arse?"

"Precisely," she said, smiling—it was obvious that she was bantering with me. "In fact, to make double sure…" She moved to a nearby table and perched on the bar stool.

"You mean I've actually got to talk to you now? But what if you're boring?"

"That's a risk you'll have to take…."

Three hours later, the risk was paying off. Despite my less than perfect start, it turned out that her arse wasn't the only thing I liked about her. She had an evil sense of humor, a natural confidence and knowing eyes, but there was a hint of vulnerability about her too. Just the occasional mannerism or thing she said made me think she was less bulletproof than she first appeared. It was only the occasional flash though, and I wasn't surprised when she was the one to ask me back to hers. Well, I was *slightly* surprised. I couldn't believe my luck. But it seemed perfectly in character for her. Of course, I wasn't going to say no. Even before I gave her an affectionate pat on the arse as we left the bar and swore I heard her moan under her breath.

Back at her flat, she got us both a beer, and sat next to me on the sofa. Away from the smoky air-conditioned bar, I could smell her properly for the first time. She had a delicate scent, albeit suffused with cigarettes and beer. But it was the musky base of her pheromones that really filled my senses: she smelled of sex. Although I was enjoying talking to her, from the second her aroma filled my nostrils, my mind was only half on her words. The rest of me was occupied with thoughts of bending her over the sofa, pushing up her skirt, ripping down her knickers and slamming my cock into her. I imagined her pushing back to meet my thrusts, my stomach slapping against her arse as I pounded her hard, unable to resist the urge to slap her bum as she begged me to go harder, faster, her muscles clenching tightly around my cock when I shot inside her.

God! I was drifting away too much. I dragged myself reluctantly back to reality. She was changing the CD and I tried to focus on what she was saying but her stereo was on the floor, so she was bending in front of me on all fours, offering me an exquisite view. I could feel my erection painfully constricted by my jeans.

"Like the view?" she said to me, looking over her shoulder. Bitch! She knew exactly what she was doing. It took every bit of willpower I had not to get on the floor and bury my face in her.

"You know I do," I said.

"How about now?" She pushed her skirt up, bunching it around her waist to reveal pale thighs clad in black hold-ups, a tiny thong all that was protecting her modesty.

I nodded, unable to trust my voice to remain steady.

"And this?" She took one of her fingers and sucked it into her mouth, keeping eye contact with me as she did so.

"If you don't stop, you're going to get what's coming to you."

"And what would that be?" She removed the finger from between her lips and, sliding her thong to the side with her other hand, pushed her finger slowly inside herself.

There's only so much a man can take and by now, it was obvious I wasn't misreading any signals.

"This," I said, and slid to the floor, pushing my face into her dripping folds. She tasted divine: sharp but with a slight sweetness too. I ran my tongue gently between her lips toward her clit, deliberately keeping the pressure light. Two could play at teasing. She pushed her arse back into my face but I kept pulling just far enough away that I was in control of how much pressure she could feel. No matter how much she wriggled, she wasn't going to get any more than I chose to give her.

"I want you," she moaned. I briefly pulled my wet face away from her.

"How much?"

"Totally. I need you inside me."

Tempting as the offer was, I was going to pay her back for her earlier game playing first.

"What would you do to have me inside you?"

"Anything."

I recognized the tone in her voice. She was at that state of arousal when nothing else matters.

"Even if I was to give you a spanking for being such a tease earlier?"

Now, there was no doubt about it. She gave a definite moan.

"God, yes. Spank me then fuck me."

Seeing her on all fours in front of me, arching her back and pushing her arse toward me, her fingers now moving over her clit, I decided to give her what she wanted. Call me a gentleman. I started with a gentle slap but, as I saw her buttocks start to get pink and felt her juices begin to run down my hand, I slapped harder, making her emit mewling cries of pleasure. Her arousal was making her inner thighs and arse sticky, and my fingers almost slipped into her center of their own accord. When I started to work my finger inside her, flicking her G-spot hard and slamming into her fast, I could feel her start to shake and knew her orgasm was imminent.

"Fuck me," she begged. "I want to feel you coming in me when I come."

My cock was aching for release so, after a few more thrusts of my fingers, I put the head of my cock at her entrance and pushed slowly into her. Every nerve in my body was screaming to slam it into her, but I wanted her to feel every inch of that first thrust, to know exactly how much she was taking and, just when she thought she'd taken me all, I'd start fucking her in earnest.

Her hips bucked back against me but I kept control, giving her my cock so slowly she was almost crying for me to hammer it into her by the time I finally buried my full length inside her. After that, all bets were off, and I began to pound her, enjoying her going wild on my cock, her muscles clenching and her entire body jerking back in an effort to take me as deep as she could. I could see her pinching her nipples as I gave her the hardest seeing-to I could remember administering in a long time. And, as I felt her telltale muscular rippling, I shot inside her, and was rewarded by her screaming in orgasm and spurting her juices onto my balls.

I stayed inside her for a while, recovering from the intensity of the orgasm, enjoying the occasional pulse that shot through her body. Then she pulled away slowly, clearly as reluctant as I was to end the fuck. She turned round and looked me in the eyes.

"Not a bad start, I guess," she said, giving me a peck on the lips.

And as she moved down my body and started to lick my wet balls, I knew the night was still young.

SHANNA GERMAIN

GOOD KITTY

KICKED TO THE CURB. That's how I feel. I've been in my cage at the rescue center for what seems like forever. But I know it's just been a day. I can't see the clock on the wall from here, but I can hear it ticking. *Tick-tick,* counting the minutes off that I'm alone, unowned. Counting the time since my master dumped me here. Traded me out for another kitty.

My neck feels bare without its collar. My throat hurts. I tell myself it's just the air in here, all the fur flying, but I know that's not the truth. I gave him four years. I wore his collar and showed off for his friends and lapped his cream. I went on kitty playdates and never minded when he decided to pet another pussy. But I would not, could not, handle it when he brought another kitty home to live with us. I tried, I did. I kept to myself, I avoided her, I tried to pretend I was just fine with it. In the end, I turned into a prissy bitch. Every time he touched her, I'd sulk in the corner. His new girl and I fought, tooth and nail, as they say, and here I am.

The front door clicks open and we all sit at attention, dogs and cats alike, as best we can in our small cages. It's a girl in black spandex, her red hair bobbed at her neck. She looks only at the kitties, poking her red nails between the bars in front of a few. When she gets to my cage, she stops. Her eyes are intensely green, catlike in their own way. I shrink to the back of my cage, feeling the wires pressed into my bare spine. She scares me, although I can't say why.

"Pretty kitty," she says, her voice a low purr. She dangles two red-tipped fingers inside the cage. "Come here, pretty kitty."

I don't want to obey—I've never had a girl master—but I don't want to be in this cage anymore either. Maybe she'll take me home, put a collar back on me. Maybe this hard-looking girl is better than another night in this cage. Better than another night alone.

I lean my head forward, just enough that she can stroke my hair. "Good girl," she says, pressing her thumb to my cheek. A shiver runs down my spine, and I feel a surprising surge of desire.

She takes her fingers out of my hair and flips up the tag on the front of my cage to read it.

"*Callie, long-haired female,*" she reads. "*Housebroken, that's good. Playful, loves lap time. Not good with dogs.*"

"Oh," she says. "It says you don't play well with other pussies either." Her eyes are back on me, that intense green, and I wonder if she's the other cat and not the master after all. "That's too bad…" She hesitates a second, as though I might correct her. But I don't. I can't. It's true. And besides, I may be a stray, I may be uncollared at the moment, but I'm not about to break rules and speak.

And then she's gone, down the row, to look at the other kitties, kitties who play well with others. I want to say something, to call her back to me, to rub up against her fingers and lick her palm. To let her know that maybe I could be okay with other pussies, to ask her to reconsider. But when I open my mouth, nothing comes out. Not even a kitten-squeak. Just silence, and the reminder that my throat aches with the kind of lonely pain that not even this green-eyed girl can fill.

I hear her talking down the row, but I can't see her from where I sit. And, before long, I have to watch while she leads another kitty, a short-haired blonde, down the aisle. They both turn to look at me, and I close my eyes.

I'm curled up on the shelter blanket, wrapped in dreams of my last master, when I hear the voices outside my cage.

"Came in last night," says a voice that I recognize. It's the woman who checked me into the shelter. "I'm surprised someone hasn't snapped her up." She lowers her voice until it's a whisper. "Someone just dumped her on our doorstep, this gorgeous girl. Can you believe it?"

"That is hard to believe," says a voice. Very male. Somehow very in control. The sound alone sends a shiver through me.

I crack one eye open, to see who's talking. All I can see are a broad pair of shoulders and a wide chest, wrapped up in a white button-down. His shirt sleeves are rolled up, showing off muscled forearms and wrists. No jewelry. He talks with his hands, fluid and confident dips and rolls.

"What's wrong with her?" the hands ask.

"Nothing as far as I can see," the woman says, her voice getting lower with each word until I can hardly hear her. "Her former master wanted another kitty in the house, it seems."

"Imagine that," he says. "I find a pussy does best if it's given undivided attention." My own pussy twitches when he says it. His fingers play along the bars of the cage, but don't enter.

I wonder if he can see me. I always thought I was pretty—my last master reassured me of that in so many ways—but now I'm not certain. Still, I want to show off my best parts, so I stretch out on the blanket, curve my hips and ass up and out. I rest my head on my hands and open my eyes, so he can see them if he looks in—I've got Siamese eyes, that blue-blue.

"Does she come when she's called?"

"Most kitties don't," she says.

"I knew there was a reason I preferred dogs." But his laugh says he doesn't mean it.

The man leans down to peer into my cage. I try to pretend I'm not looking, that I don't care, but I catch a glimpse of salt-and-pepper hair, dark brown eyes framed by tortoiseshell glasses. A little scruff around his face, but it's nice, and thin lips. He looks nothing like my last master, which makes me both excited and nervous.

His fingers come through the bars, wiggle in the air at me.

"Hey there, sweet girl," he says, like he's known me all his life. I sniff his fingers; they smell like cedar and sweet cream.

"Come here," he whispers. I think about his question of whether kitties come when they're called. I always do—did—for my last master.

I like that feeling of doing what I'm told. So when he calls a second time, with "Here, kittykittykitty," I move close enough so that he can reach me through the bars. When he buries his fingers in my hair, it's just hard enough. I rub myself against him, loving the pressure of his strong fingers against the back of my neck.

"Oh, yes, you're such a good girl," he says. "Aren't you?"

I'm getting wet just listening to him talk. When he stops moving his fingers, I butt up against him with my head until he starts again.

The woman clears her throat. "We do have private playrooms where kitties and their potential owners can get acquainted," she says. "Would you like to take her there and see if the two of you are a good fit?"

I hold my breath as he rubs my head with a little less pressure. Will he say yes? Or will he, too, decide he doesn't want me and move on to another kitty?

"What do you think, sweet girl?" he asks. I rub against his fingers, trying to convince him to say yes.

He pinches my earlobe between his fingernails and I let out a little yowl of surprise.

"Maybe later," he says. I look up at him, surprised and hurt, but he's already taken his fingers away and is moving down the row.

After that, I don't know what to do. No master's going to take me home. I'll be stuck here forever. I'll grow old watching other masters come and pick out cute kitties. I lie down on my blanket and close my eyes, trying not to cry. Every time I swallow, I feel exposed. I want to go home.

A couple of hours later, the nice woman who rescued me opens my cage.

"C'mon little one," she says. "Let's go." She holds out a collar that says AFRS on the side. That's where I am, the rescue shelter. If I put that collar on, does it mean the shelter owns me? Does it mean they've given up hope that I'll ever be rescued? I cower against the back bars.

"It's okay," she says, her voice soothing me. "It's just temporary."

She clicks it around my neck. I'm ashamed to wear this collar and to be on the end of her leash—the AFRS printed on both basically tell the world, "Dumped kitty walking here." But I follow her down the aisle.

Outside a door, she leans down to take the collar off.

"Go on in," she says, holding the door open for me.

I go through it, and it's him. The man from before. He's bigger than I thought, tall, and his shoulders are wide. In front of him, he's laid out a blanket. I can tell it's his, because it doesn't say AFRS on it, and because when I step on it, it's way softer than the one in my cage. There are two bowls, empty, that look too clean to belong to the shelter. And on the table beside him, a black bag. But the thing that catches my eye is the leash and collar set in front of it. Dark purple. Brand new, and set with little silver slivers. I can already feel it against my skin. My throat has never felt so naked, so vulnerable. My heart too. Maybe he'll take me after all.

"Come here, sweet girl," he says. "Sorry to make you wait, but I needed to get a few things."

I crawl up to him and wonder what to do now. My old master always wanted me to rub my head against his shins, but I don't know if this is what he wants. So I wait to be told.

Without saying anything, he steps to the side of me. He just looks. Quiet, and for a long time. I arch my back for him, and drop down onto my forearms. And then he steps beside me and does the same thing. My pussy feels him watching and it wants to hide, but I force myself to stay still and let him look.

He runs a hand over my head and down my back. When he gets to my ass, he squeezes it and then gives it a little smack. It doesn't hurt, but it's loud. I don't even jump.

"I don't know," he says. "You seem awfully well behaved. I wonder what you could have done to end up here?"

This is a trick, I know. To see if I'll act out, or give him an answer. I stay totally still, on my knees and forearms, waiting to see what he'll do.

He squats down behind me and runs his fingers down my thighs on the outside. Just his fingertips, with enough pressure that I wonder if my skin turns even whiter beneath his touch. He strokes the back of my thighs, moving closer and closer to my center.

"Pretty pussy," he says and I think he means me, but also he means the part of me that he's almost touching. That I so badly want him to touch. He's so close I can feel his breath against my skin.

I lean back into his fingers, asking for it. Please.

"Oh no," he says. His fingers go away, and he stands. I can't hear anything from behind me, and I don't dare look. I worry that I've ruined it, that he's going to take me back to that cage.

Footsteps, and then he's in front of me. Without looking at me, he picks the black bag off the table, and disappears again. I hear the clasp of the bag, the paper and something soft all rubbing together. The sounds excite me, even though I don't know what they are.

He touches his fingers to the bottom of my pussy, not on my clit, but close. And then he shows me how wet I am by sliding two fingers inside me. I clench around his fingers, to try and keep them there, but he just laughs and pulls them out.

"My, you are a greedy girl," he says. "If I didn't know better, I'd think you'd been a stray for a long time."

I smell the lube before I feel it, and my body responds. My nipples tighten against the blanket, and my pussy starts a slow pound that I wonder if he can see.

Then I feel it—he's lubed a dildo, and he's twisting it into me like a corkscrew. I'm so wet that I doubt he needed lube, but I like the sound it makes, the kind of slow squish as it enters me. When the dildo's all the way in, he taps the end of it. I'm so full I feel that little tap all the way down inside me.

He presses something small and hard against my ass, and I raise my head in surprise. I nearly look back at him over my shoulder, but I stop myself.

Still, he sees.

"You can look," he says. "All good kitties need a tail, don't you think?"

I look over my shoulder. He holds a small black butt plug with a long kitty tail attached. The color matches my hair. I'd never had one before, and I can't wait to see how it looks. I arch my butt in the air, to tell him that it's perfect.

I watch him as he slides it inside me. Even lubed up, it's big, bigger than I'm used to, and he goes slow, letting my body open up to the pressure. I feel it filling me up, until I'm not sure I can take any more. And then it's all the way in. It gives me a perfect tail, long and sleek. I twitch my ass, which makes the tail bat back and forth and wiggles the butt plug and the dildo inside me.

He laughs. "I'm glad you like it." With both hands, he strokes my tail. The butt plug hits all my pressure points, and I'm afraid I'm going to come. I make a long, low sound, half squeak, half meow, and turn back to the front. I can't watch anymore.

He walks around to the front of me, his hand trailing over my ass and up my back as he goes. He unzips his jeans so slowly I can hear each of the teeth as they come apart.

"Most kitties I know love cream," he says. I try not to feel my heart stutter when he says that. Does he know a lot of kitties? I don't want the answer.

He slides his jeans and underwear down. God, he's gorgeous there too. Slim hips and muscular thighs. And then his cock. It sticks out from under his button-down, long and wide, and I want to lick it. I want to see what he tastes like, to know what it would be like to have him fill my mouth the way I'm filled everywhere else.

He puts his hands in my hair again, that just-right pressure until I'm practically purring against him.

"How about you, sweet girl?" he asks. He makes a ring around his cock with his fingers, offers it to me.

I touch my tongue to my top lip. Yes please.

"Go ahead," he says. I lean forward and touch my tongue to the base of his cock. He tastes of clean salt and wood, something fragrant. Pine or cedar. I lap at it while he holds himself out to me, following the veins that snake just beneath the skin. It's so hard I can feel the skin stretching around it.

I take just the tip between my lips and run my tongue over the smooth bulb there. He moans, and the sound makes me clench around all the things he's put inside me.

He pushes all the way into my mouth, and I take as much of him as I can. It feels so good to feel him pulsing on my tongue. I suck him, hard and then soft, taking little nibbles sometimes, until his breath gets harsh and ragged. Precum coats my tongue and I lap it up, playing the tip of my tongue around his hole. I suck on the shirttails that hang on either side of his cock, letting my tongue feel the rough fabric. With the fabric on my tongue, I lick him again, just to see if he likes the way it feels, like a wet kitty tongue. He hisses between his teeth and his cock jumps.

When I take all of him inside my mouth again, he puts his hands around my throat. Not hard, but like a temporary collar. Like a way to claim me for now. The thought makes me so wet I can feel the dildo start to slide out of me.

"Don't let it," he says. And I clench my pussy hard to keep it in. I know it won't stay for long, so I'm grateful when he moans and arches against me. "Don't stop," he says. "I want to give you my cream. I want you to lick it all up."

His cock pulses in my mouth and then he floods me. He tastes salty, but sweet, and I wonder if he ate something just for me, to make it taste like that. I swallow it all, and then lick every drop from him. I nestle my tongue in his balls, and lick him until he's clean.

He pulls up his pants, and sits in the chair in front of me. "You're such a good, good, pussy," he says. "Do you want to come home with me?"

Before I can answer, he dangles the collar in the air, and I swipe at it, but miss, which makes him laugh.

"Do you think you want this?" he asks.

He holds it out in front of me, a hand on each end, so it's flat. All I'd have to do is put my neck on that strip of leather and I would be his.

"Don't say yes unless you're sure," he says. "I don't have any other pussies. You'll be my only one, but I'm not always as nice a master as I was today."

I'm counting on that. I stretch my neck out until I can feel the leather collar against the bottom of my neck. He wraps the leather around my skin. The buckle makes a small metallic sound as he fastens it. When I swallow, I feel the smooth weight of the leather against my throat.

"Now you're mine for a long time, sweet girl," he says.

I sure hope so.

THOMAS S. ROCHE

PARTS OF HEAVEN

K ATE LEFT ME NOT SO LONG AGO—a year, two years, I forget. It was lonely until I found Angel. Kate still calls sometimes, leaves friendly little messages about mutual acquaintances on my voice mail at work. I rarely return them.

Angel's got curves that stretch from Heaven to Hell by way of Purgatory. You can lose yourself in those curves, slide your body against them and feel it giving way. Her whispers of invitation draw you in and twist your mind until there's nothing left but devotion. That's why I love her so. She's got shiny chrome running from front to back, a tight little rear end that holds its own even when you're riding it hotter and harder and faster than seems possible. She's got a bright little tailpipe that gives off a low rumble, and buffed-leather kisses against your ass.

She talks to me as I ride her. She whispers rosaries of devotion under her breath. She burns somewhere, deep under those seductive curves. I can disappear inside her, vanish into her fine softness like I never existed in the first place. I love to run my hands over her surfaces, feeling how she responds to my touch. I love to explore her like a patient on my table; I love to race her uphill, downhill, hearing her moan low in her throat, pushing her harder, harder, until she can't take any more and then pushing her just a little farther.

She moves like a phantom, a goddess—an angel.

In my professional life I am a priest, the high priest of surgical transfiguration. It's not a job, or at least I don't think of it that way, any more than I think of Angel as a mode of transportation. More appropriately, it's a calling, perhaps even a religion. I sometimes think I was given the opportunity to become something not quite human, something so much more—to aspire to godhood, or perhaps merely to be a priest at the temple of modern medicine. I work the miracles of the gods; I take people apart and put them back together again in accordance with their wishes. Day by day by day people come to me broken, twisted, destroyed. I create them anew.

My skills at the surgeon's table have increased since I fell for Angel. She has much to teach me about the structure of the body. Often as my fingers work deftly inside the body of a patient, as I intently restructure the patient to better fit her or his needs, I meditate on the beauty of Angel and all she has to offer me. Surgery has treated me well, given me the money to indulge in such lovers as Angel. But Angel has made me a better surgeon than I could ever have been without her.

I take her apart on the weekends, reverently placing her insides on silken white cloths arranged as on an altar across the driveway of my four-bedroom house. I reach inside her and touch all the surfaces of her engine, experience her perfection. I run my hands along her driveshaft; I stroke her pistons, caress her block. I explore the intricacies of her fuel assembly, delicately massage her oil filter. My neighbors sometimes wonder why I take her apart every weekend; the CPA across the street asked me, one Saturday, if Angel was British or something. British. What a quaint thought. "She is Italian," I told him with a sneer.

As the breeze cuts across the driveway, I explore each piece I have laid reverently on the cloths upon concrete. My fascination gives way to bewilderment, that machinery should be so superior to cruel, sad flesh—flesh, that is the eyes and the ears of the soul and the conscience of the universe; flesh, that is the knowledge and the love and the understanding of the cosmos; flesh, that withers and decays and becomes nothing; flesh, that vanishes not unlike the timing on an Alfa Romeo— but the Alfa is superior in the cult of modern love, for machinery has interchangeable parts.

My article in the *Journal of Surgery* brings a torrent of international scorn and international praise. I am invited to give the keynote address at a small but prestigious surgery conference this spring, in a city just a short flight away. In my acceptance letter I ask them to add the cost of the ticket to my honorarium.

Some weekends, after I've explored Angel's delights, exposed her delicious insides, socketed her parts together, tightened her screws, polished her chrome, I need to bring her inside the three-car garage for a little while. There I touch her again, with love and tenderness and more than a little ardor, and behind the garage doors our transgressions meet each other in the caress of petrochemical fantasies. If I could bring her to the bedroom with me, I would tangle her up in my satin sheets, would spread her out across the expanse of the king-sized waterbed and penetrate her, hearing her moan and rumble and squeal as I ride her. But I must content myself with touching her in the garage, for not even Sharper Image makes a bed big enough for my lover. I remove my clothes and feel her smooth metal against me. I weep as she holds me, and for a time our parts are interchangeable.

Nights like that, I take her through the city streets, through the lights and the drifting clouds of crack smoke, through the scattered bombed-out buildings, the crowds of derelicts and the haunted faces of the damned. There's a street I like where six theaters come together on a couple of corners, where you can take your pick of the lovely flesh under the slanted light. I drive my white Angel, and the sight of her with the top down draws them over to run their hands over her curves and coo about how beautiful she is and oh, is she Italian?

Angel loves all this attention. The girls shake and jiggle and promise me all sorts of lovely things. I flash a few twenties and their feeding frenzy turns the waters of the district to a red-light froth.

After I've chosen one, I usually drive up into the hills, where I can park on a secluded ridge, leaving the top down. There I can look out over the city and the bay and feel the breeze cutting across my body while the guest leans down in the car and does her work. I like to think of these as threesomes, my understanding being that Angel, in her infinite understanding, holds me so dear that she will share me with other lovers. So that when I come, she is happy.

Some nights, I take two lovers up there. They think it's a little strange, maybe, but cash is cash and I'm always careful not to troll in the rich neighborhoods, where the girls will be less impressed with Angel. I ask one girl to undress and stretch on Angel's hood while the second ministers to me. There's something deliciously intimate for Angel about the beauty of a half-naked young prostitute writhing and moaning, stretched out on her hood, while I ejaculate copiously into the mouth of another.

Other days I take her for long drives over the hills; I know places where she can show me her stuff for hours. I know she wants to come, wants to hit 100, 120, 130 on the open road, her supposedly street-legal engine roaring with a terrible authority. At that speed, the ride is still smooth, but every tiny bump in the road is like a spasmodic jerk of her pleasure. I rock up and down, feeling the rumble of her engine against my ass. My cock is hard in my pants, and as my body bounces up and down in her soft seats, Angel reaches her second wind, picking up speed and screaming faster and faster. Then I let myself go, filling my pants with a seed that, if there were any justice in this universe, could mix with Angel's transmission fluid and produce a child half of skin, half of machinery, all of beauty; a child of steel and/or flesh, and more than a little love.

Sometimes I end up in Barstow or Santa Barbara and have to get a hotel. I'm not as young as I used to be.

I cruise the streets, hungry for flesh. I want three tonight, three girls who will make love to Angel and me with a fervor unmatched. But I want something new, something different; I take a left and head down to a slightly different section of the red-light district. Here the flesh is further decayed: sorrier—or cheaper, more vulnerable. This excites me somehow. I pull up alongside a trio of hookers.

"Ooooooooh, look at Doctor Love," says one, leaning down and showing me her breasts. "Take me for a ride, sugar, I *love* independent suspension!"

"A car like this makes my pussy wet," says the second in a lustful growl, climbing onto Angel's hood and making eyes at me through the windshield. "I'm dripping on your Armor-All."

"You like Alfa Romeo?" whispers the third, a blonde, bending low and whispering hot breath into my ear, her tongue drawing inviting circles as she takes my hand and put it down her shirt to feel the hard swell of her breast . "How about Hoover?"

I pause for a moment. How did the first one know I'm a doctor? Ah, of course. The cover story of the *Medical News and Review*. She recognized me from my picture. It's satisfying to know that Angel and I will be with a prostitute who keeps up on the medical literature.

I cram all three of the hookers into Angel's single passenger seat and we head into the hills as they tell me all the things they're going to do to me. The conversation degenerates as I bring Angel up the hill, and by the time we park they're trading makeup tips with occasional muttered promises of "We'll do you right" and "Gonna give you some lovin'." Leticia is the name of the talkative one. "Nurse Leticia, Angel and Sweet Simone got a new patient, Doc, he gonna get the best care around. Get that pad out, Doctor, write yourself a script for satis-FAC-shun!!!" She snaps her finger and put her lips close to mine. "Three hefty doses!!"

It's a warm night. It takes some extra cash, but I get the two of them onto Angel's hood and tell them to caress her. Rub their hardened nipples against her smoothness. The third, the dark-haired girl, gets to do the work because her name is Angel. There's something achingly beautiful about that.

"So long and stiff," she says, rolling a rubber down my shaft, rubbing my cock over her face. Angel takes my cock into her mouth, and while Angel sucks me, Leticia and Simone squirm on the hood of the car playing with each other's tits. I think they've misunderstood—they think I want to see a girl-girl show, like the kind I could see any night at the Sixth Street Theater.

"The car," I rasp. "Touch the car!"

"What?" says Leticia, cocking her head.

"Touch the car! Stroke it!"

The two of them must stare at me for a minute, then look down at Angel, then back at me, then at Angel. Uncomprehending.

"You're kinky," says Leticia. "I appreciate that in a medical professional."

Both she and Simone begin to touch Angel halfheartedly, but when they see my response their enthusiasm increases. Soon they're humping violently against Angel, fucking her with their legs spread. Leticia yanks down her top and pulls up one of the windshield wipers, sliding it between her ample tits. She pushes them together and moans "Ooooooh baby" as she slides the wiper in and out of the tight channel of flesh.

"Oh God, yes," I groan, reaching for the washer button.

I hit the button and washer fluid shoots all over Leticia's tits. Leticia goes along with it, lets out a little moan, rubs the fluid all over her tits until it soaks her shirt. She holds on to the wiper as it flops back and forth, in and out between her tits. I hear a sharp crack and Leticia gets this look over her face like she's really fucked up. I almost come right then, seeing the limp windshield wiper flapping around over and between her breasts. "Whoops—" Leticia starts to say, but I shriek "Don't worry about it! Don't stop! Don't stop! Goddamn it, don't stop!" and so she goes back to riding the broken wiper while I lean on the washer button and fluid sprays across her belly and breasts and face, making her makeup run. It's not easy, but I manage to hold back, letting out wild moans of pleasure and pistoning my hips. Simone has just been watching with this look of bewilderment on her face, but now she gets the idea. She sort of shrugs and then plants herself on the other washer, sliding her ass up to the front of Angel's hood and hiking her spandex skirt up as far as it will go. She spreads her legs around the wiper and rides it, moaning, rides it until it cracks, and the washer cables squirt all over her exposed crotch.

I catch a beautiful vision of black lace panties—and as the washer fluid soaks them they become slightly transparent. My eyes go wide. It seems like my brain was playing tricks on me there for a second.

Simone can't match Leticia's enthusiasm, though; Leticia has it down pat. She smears the washer fluid all over her body, whimpering things like "Oh babycakes, wash *me*," and "Whoa, sugarplum, make it the *SPIN* cycle." She runs out of things to say after a while, though, and just starts moaning, prompting Simone to let out a halfhearted "Wipe me down!" It's not the second-rate dialogue, though, that's getting me off, it's the sight of Angel—my Angel—working the two whores, shooting warm fluid on them and flapping between their tits.

I'm groaning and rocking up and down, pumping my hips back and forth while Angel rides me like a vixen. I start to whimper. I throw my head back and almost scream, the hottest orgasm of my life exploding through my cock and into Angel's mouth. I shudder and thrash back and forth, and Angel holds on for dear life, her lips clamped around the head of my cock as she milks me. Finally, my spasms subside and my head slumps forward.

I am greeted by the sight of Simone and Leticia, half-naked, covered in washer-fluid lather, their clothes and hair soaked, regarding me as if I were the most extreme kind of maniac.

The washers emit a rhythmic clicking sound, spent.

Angel looks up at me from my lap with pretty much the same expression on her face.

"You get the prize, Doc. Weirdest trick I ever turned."

"Me, too," says Angel, wiping her mouth as she slips the condom off and tosses it away. "You don't even have any competition."

"Yeah, same here," says Simone, nodding her head vigorously as she tucks her tits back into her soaked lace top. "I think there ought to be some sort of award for this kind of stuff."

"Congratulations," says Leticia matter-of-factly. "You got first fucking place. I hope you got cash to pay for these fuckin' clothes you ruined."

After a long session of cleanup with chamois cloths from the trunk, I drive the girls back to the district slowly, savoring the sharp, soapy smell of washer fluid, tasting the ripeness of my union with Angel. I drop them off where I got them, and they shuffle away, my cash tucked into their boots.

Except Leticia. I put my hand out and stop her.

"What is it, sugar? You want my phone number? Hey, you *know* where to find Lady Leticia." She indicates the streets with a wave of her hand.

"No," I say. "It's not that. I just wondered…"

She leans forward. "How I keep my girlish figure? Where I get my creamy skin? How an old broad like me can exude such a raw, primal sensuality?"

"No, it's not that," I say. "I just wondered…"

"Spit it out, Doc, time costs money."

"How did you knew I was a doctor?

She smiles. "See you in the clinic on Tuesday morning, Doc. Maybe you could tell your nurse to sport me a free shot this time? Make another trip out here Tuesday night, see if it makes a difference." She winks at me.

I put Angel in gear. Leticia shrugs, tugs at her bra straps, and vanishes into the dark and the drifts of smoke, calling "Love for sale, oh baby love for sale—ooooh, a Caddy, I *love* Caddies…." I hit the gas and everything goes away.

I have surgery to perform the next morning. I lie awake tangled in the satin sheets, the waterbed rocking me to sleep. I distract myself by dreaming of the new windshield wipers I'll get for Angel—the best money can buy. Gold-plated, perhaps?

The distractions subside and I look up at the mirrored ceiling, eyes wide, gently rocking on the warm plastic waves.

Of course, Angel was the only one who actually touched me. Maybe she was different. Maybe she was just along for the ride.

It seems impossible. I've been in the field for long enough…I should have recognized the signs.

After years of holy service as the high priest of gender reassignment, taking people apart and putting them together again…I should have understood. Why didn't I? After years of my work, learning the lessons of Angel and of my patients—I should already know the answer to any questions posed in prayer. But things are not like I thought they were. Machine and mind, steel and/or flesh, an Alfa Romeo and a third-rate streetwalker…they're not as different as I thought they were. In the scattered wreckage of the millennium, we find gods and goddesses among whatever is left. We all inhabit different parts of heaven. We fit pieces of our lives, sometimes broken pieces, together to form what passes as a whole—and it is *only* through change, through assemblage, that a functioning whole can be created.

The holy belief that flesh and therefore life is mutable is whispered like a prayer or a mantra on the stainless-steel and starched white altar, the white linoleum prayer mat, with me as the priest, reciting the liturgy with my scalpel and my hands. So as the unwilling holy man of such a movement, it only makes sense that I should sample its communion wine. Offering my devotion unto the god of medical transfiguration.

And all God's children have interchangeable parts.

— 125 —

ALISON TYLER

BLADES

K NIVES AREN'T EASY. They're more difficult, say, than palming an apple, the rounded red fruit cupped under your hand in an arc as you slide between the automatic glass doors of the neighborhood grocery. Far more complicated than lifting a lipstick. Those short, cylindrical tubes always fit so easily beneath the edge of a cuff before disappearing up the sleeve in a reverse magic trick. Trust me, knives take skill. And more than that, they take will. You have to want to steal that shiny, mirrored blade, to conceal it carefully, so that you don't cut yourself to bits in the process.

The cutting, of course, comes later.

That said, I'm the type of girl who gets an intense rush from any type of thievery. From absconding successfully with a single piece of fruit that I know I'll never eat to taking lipsticks and glosses and tints that simply gather dust on my bathroom shelf. The art of stealing is enough.

It transforms me. A heart-pounding energy fills my brain when I realize that, fuck yes, I'm going to do it once again. I'm going to walk out of this store with something that I haven't paid for. Fear freezes into a pleasing numbness as I grip an item tightly and make my way to the nearest exit.

But knives are the best, because blades turn me on.

I've been at the game for a number of years. I know what I'm doing. You'd never guess my sexual hobby from looking at me. I've mastered the nonchalant expression that I wear as I cruise the cutlery section of a gourmet cooking store. I'm no cat burglar. You won't find me robbing a place after hours, scuttling through deserted racks of silverware accompanied only by my shadow and the red light on the video camera overhead. What's the fun in that? I like the challenge of working when there are people present. Security guards. Overly attentive shopgirls. And other customers. *Especially* other customers. Those housewives who trundle along after a new paring knife, one with a handle that won't break off this time, thank you very much. The atrocious newlyweds exchanging a set of butter knives for a fancy blade that will cut through the slimy seaweed skin of homemade sushi.

"We're making it ourselves," they gush in saccharine-sweet voices, eyes on each other rather than the prices of the expensive weapons displayed before them.

But my eyes are focused on the razor-sharp edges that can do such damage in the hands of those less experienced, and even more damage in the hands of those who know what they're doing. I like the high-end knives, often imported from Europe, with black handles made of heavy-duty rubber. Usually, these blades are trapped behind glass. You have to ask for permission to touch.

"That one," I nod to the helpful pink-cheeked salesgirl. "The small one."

I get wet as soon as the slick rubber meets the flesh of my palm. My thumb works up the edge slowly, to dance lightly over the ridge of the blade. It's a tango between steel and flesh, and flesh, I know, will always lose. In my head, I can already visualize the heartbreakingly lovely hue of that first drop of blood. Cherry red, the little pinprick of liquid will dot and then swell, blooming—

"Oh, gosh, Miss," the honey-blonde salesgirl murmurs. "You've cut yourself."

And I have, which is shocking, to me as much as to her. I've never done something like this before. Never let myself slip up so badly in public. She is rightly concerned, taking me firmly by the wrist, hurrying the two of us to a back room, where I see a half-filled coffeemaker, a box of donuts that grow staler as I watch. My dark brown eyes are clear and sharp. Everything is in perfect focus. That line of blood as it trickles now, pooling—

"Raise up your arm," she says, lifting my hand to show me what she wants me to do as she rummages a cabinet in search of bandages. The knife, I discover, is still in my other hand, and I slide it secretly into my pocket without thinking. Blade first. Down my thigh. If I sit, I'll stab myself.

"Here we go." Her voice is calm, and I recognize in it the exact same tone that the nurse at my pediatrician's office always used before bringing out the shot. "It'll sting," she warns, "but only for a moment."

Rubbing alcohol is poured in a clear river on a puffball of cotton. I don't feel the pain as the girl swipes the damp fluff across my thumb.

My head tilts back and I look at her. Soft golden hair, a wisp over her forehead that she blows out of the way with an exasperated breath. Flushed cheeks, dark gray eyes, lips colored as red as that first drop of blood against my pale skin. She notices me watching, but says nothing, applying pressure, careful and steady. I'm sure that she'll take out a Band-Aid next, warn me about my carelessness before ushering me back into the real world of the busy store.

"What did you take the last time?" she asks, surprising me so greatly that I take a step back from her. I don't get far because she hasn't let go of my wrist. She's holding tight, and her eyes, not just gray now but the flat color of wet pavement, are gazing fiercely into my own. "It was a display knife, I think," she says, nodding in agreement with her own statement. "Am I right?"

Her fingers grip tightly into my wrist, holding on to my pulse point. I can feel my heart pounding where skin meets skin. There's the sound of a fire burning in my head. Rustling. White noise. I'm so confused that I can't speak.

"A Classe, from Italy," she says next, and the name is like a dirty word to me. Something hot and exciting. *Talk to me about knives*, I want to whisper to her. *Describe the rough edges of a serrated blade. The sleek lines of a parer. Whisper longingly to me about my favorites: the little ones, sharp and dangerous, like the dagger in my pocket.*

"I saw you," she says now. "And I waited for you to come back. I knew you couldn't stay away."

She'll turn me in, I think, picturing my first arrest ever. I see myself taken somewhere stark and frightening where I'll have to confess. I stole an apple, I remember. That was my first time. Lifted the sweet, ripe fruit from the pyramid of Washington red globes and got away before anyone could see. *I took a lipstick next,* I imagine myself saying—the words will pour from my lips in a rush. No one will be able to stop me. I took a lipstick, and then I wrote twisted things on my bathroom mirror. Perverted fantasies that looked as if they were etched on that frozen glass in blood.

"The back way," she says, "follow me."

I move without thinking, having to do as she says since she still hasn't released me from her powerful grip. As we hurry down the metal stairs of an employee exit, I notice the fresh scent of her shampoo, the sweet smell of her skin. Then we are suddenly in bright sunlight, walking out of the mall and to the parking lot. She takes me to a pickup truck, shiny and black, and soon we're inside together, on the leather seats. I squirm slightly, so as not to sever anything serious with my hidden prize. Simply knowing the knife is still in my pocket gives me strength.

Speaking in a voice that sounds nothing like my own, I hear myself giving directions to my apartment. I understand that when we get there, she'll see my loot. The blades in a row on a metal board, all of them pinned up there like prized butterflies in a lepidopterist's collection. This vision turns me on more than I can describe.

In silence, we drive the short distance to my place, and once she parks the truck, we move quickly from the empty street to the stark metal stairs to the bare patch of concrete outside my front door. My hands shake as I fumble with the key, until finally I make it work in the lock, and then we're inside in my Spartan living room staring at each other. Without a word, she reaches into my pocket and comes up with the stolen goods. I sigh as I see her fingers close around the handle.

It's like watching a porno movie, something sexual and tangible, raw and rough. And then she's turning me, slicing easily through the thin fabric of my long-sleeved black T-shirt. Tracing the very tip of the blade against my naked skin. Not cutting. Just letting me know how it's going to feel.

And it's going to feel like this—

Magically, the light grows brighter. Objects so often fuzzy in my vision take on clean edges. The knife presses harder and I hear my skin humming with the precursor to true pain, the only thing that clarifies my life and makes me come. She's talking now. I hear bits of sentences. While my vision is brighter, my hearing is focused only on the sound that a blade makes when it kisses skin. But I get snippets, and I make out certain key words: *Waited. Searched. Needed.* She needed to meet me as desperately as I needed to get caught.

There is an artistry to what she's doing. Teasing me with that sharp, true point of my favorite sex toy: a knife. I'm contained in my black jeans, black boots, shreds of fabric that once made up my shirt. My long, gleaming dark hair is in a high ponytail off my neck. I can feel her breath on my skin, and I sense the moment before she presses harder. Before she brings the pain home where I will really be able to feel it. I hold myself steady, feeling the wetness seep from between my nether lips, and I realize that stealing is nothing compared to this. The rush of taking something pales against the experience of being caught. And being punished.

The blade connects. My eyes close. My chin lifts.

With each flinty metal bite against my skin, my cunt contracts firmly. It pulses with a strong, regular rhythm, beats as if it has a heart of its own. In a flash, I know that if she works me long enough, hard enough, I will need nothing else. Pain enhances pleasure in the wet heat between my thighs. There is a perfect bliss each time she touches unmarked flesh. Every stolen item I've ever hidden away in my clothes has been practice for this.

She says, "Strip for me now. I want you naked."

As she steps back to give me room, I peel off my jeans for her, feeling my hand trembling at the button fly. Where is my calmness? Shivers ripple through me, but I manage to obey her command. In seconds, I'm nude, my clothes a discarded pile on the floor. Then I wait. She walks around me, observing in silence, and finally she comes forward and kisses me on the lips. Once. Again, I smell the different fragrances of her body that combine into one sweet scent. Breathtaking, almost overpowering. I close my eyes, drinking her in. With a single gesture, she demonstrates for me that she knows everything I want. Holding the blade in her hand, she gently rests the flat edge of it against my cheek, letting me feel the cold steel on my hot skin. I concentrate on that feeling, learning it, memorizing it.

Bending in front of me on her knees, she uses her free hand to part my pussy lips and she presses her mouth to my cunt, tasting me almost casually with a probing thrust of her tongue. A lick. A flicker of her wetness against my wetness. She's searching, quickly finding out how excited I am already, in the short space of time, from the teasing lines alone of the blade on my back.

The knife is still in her hand, and as she presses her lips against my waiting cunt, she starts to trace again, to sketch designs with the point of it. To illustrate for me how well she knows her craft. A blade pressed firmly into skin will leave a white mark, a momentary etching that lasts for several fleeting seconds without breaking the skin. Try it yourself. Drag one nail against the back of your hand and see how pretty the lines can look. They quickly fade. Too quickly. In order to make them last, you have to use something else. Something serious.

I look down and see her working the knife along my inner thighs, taking her time. She will mark me all over, I think. She will plan and diagram and then make the first cut. Can I wait? That's the question. The only question.

In the full-length windows across the room, I see the mirrored reflection of the two of us. I am naked; she is clothed. Her blonde hair is still in her face, effectively pushed out of her eyes every second or two with a practiced puff of her breath. My sleek, slim body appears so well-contained in comparison. Everything about me—my pale skin, dark hair, deep brown eyes—radiates an inner cool, a quiet steadiness. Cutting through that surface shell will finally release me.

She works me steadily, alternating between the teasing lines of the blade against my flesh and crimson-smeared kisses with her parted mouth. The sensations match each other in their ability to thrill me. Her wet warm tongue trips between my parted pussy lips, spreading me open, pushing me wide. Her tongue makes circles, then diamonds, up and over my clit. A whisper-soft tickle, gently, so gently, followed by a more resounding lap of the flat of her tongue. Alternating motions have me groaning fiercely. And I shudder and bite down on the sounds that threaten to escape.

"Tell me," she says, her breath a rush of warmth against my wetness.

"Tell you what?" I beg.

"Confess—"

I close my eyes tighter. I can hear the words in my head. It's all about the wanting. Not possessing. Not owning. But the wanting before. And the knowing that I can have whatever I need if I only have the strength to take it. Yet all I manage to whisper are those last words. "Take it—"

"Look at me," she insists, and I open my eyes and stare down at her. "That's what you'll do," she agrees, sounding pleased. "You'll take it for me. Whatever I have to give. Everything I have to give."

Then suddenly I feel the handle of the blade slipped up inside me. She's holding the sharp razor edge in her hand, carefully cradling the scissor-sharp point as she fucks me with the thick rubber handle. Fucks me hard and seriously. I'm filled by this tool. For once, I'm filled. Does the need lessen? Does the wanting evaporate?

No. Insert a bitter laugh here. No. I just want it more.

In and out, she works the knife within me, pumping her fist against me. I think about that knife concealed in the fleshy softness of her palm. I imagine that her fingers will close tightly—too tightly— around the dagger, and I see in my head the lines that the knife will make. Pure ruby red liquid squeezing through her fist as she continues to thrust that handle inside me, such a true crimson river that it will seem fake. This is the mental picture that takes me right up to the edge.

"Talk to me," she says again. "Make it real."

"It's a rush," I whisper to her, trying to explain. "It's all about the rush."

Lowering my head to my chest, I start to come. Steady, so steady, causing no sudden movements, the ripples spread through me. So sweetly and quietly those waves spread outward again and again as if they'll never stop. But when I see my reflection in the mirror, I am unsurprised to see that I remain poker-faced. Emotionless. Unchanged until she pulls the knife away from my body, surveys the area of her desire, and makes the first true cut. Only then, when there is no going back, can I give in to her, allowing myself to be caught. And in doing so, allowing myself finally to get free.

ABOUT THE EDITOR

CALLED A "LITERARY SIREN" by Good Vibrations, Alison Tyler is naughty and she knows it. She is the author of more than twenty explicit novels, including *Rumors*, *Tiffany Twisted,* and *With or Without You* (all published by Cheek), and the winner of "best kinky sex scene" as awarded by Scarlet Magazine. Her novels and short stories have been translated into Japanese, Dutch, German, Italian, Norwegian, Greek, and Spanish.

According to *Clean Sheets*, "Alison Tyler has introduced readers to some of the hottest contemporary erotica around." And she's done so through the editing of more than thirty-five sexy anthologies, including the erotic alphabet series published by Cleis Press; as well as the *Naughty Stories from A to Z* series, the *Down & Dirty* series, *Naked Erotica*, and *Juicy Erotica* (all from Pretty Things Press). Please drop by www.prettythingspress.com.

Ms. Tyler is loyal to coffee (black), lipstick (red), and tequila (straight). She has tattoos, but no piercings; a wicked tongue, but a quick smile; and bittersweet memories, but no regrets. She believes it won't rain if she doesn't bring an umbrella, prefers hot and dry to cold and wet, and loves to spout her favorite motto: "You can sleep when you're dead." She chooses Led Zeppelin over the Beatles, the Cure over NIN, and the Stones over everyone—yet although she appreciates good rock, she has a pitiful weakness for '80s hair bands. In all things important, she remains faithful to her partner of more than a decade, but she still can't settle on one perfume. Visit www.alisontyler.com for more luscious revelations or myspace.com/alisontyler, if you'd like to be her friend.